Also by Gaia Servadio

MELINDA

Salomé

&

Don Giovanni

Translated by L. K. Conrad

Gaia Servadio

Salomé

NOTES FOR A NEW NOVEL

Don Giovanni

NOTES FOR A REVISED OPERA

NEW YORK

FARRAR, STRAUS & GIROUX

1969

Contents

✿

Salomé

∴

NOTES FOR A NEW NOVEL

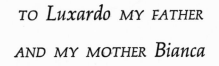

TO *Luxardo* MY FATHER

AND MY MOTHER *Bianca*

Salomé

❦❦❦❦❦❦❦❦❦❦❦

"I wish that you'd have to." He has the strangest way of talking. I must come up with a name for this character. Names are the hardest part of writing novels. If I call him Marco or Carlo, it makes him an Italian; Charles or Peter and he's a common Englishman. The nationality shouldn't be definite, nor the setting or time. Remember to have a look in the mythological dictionary and in *Who's Who*. How about calling him "Q." for now.

"Would you mind telling me what to do?" demands the heroine.

The same problem with her. She needs a decent name. It ought to be a bit old-fashioned, a name people have already used quite a lot that she will make unique. God no, not Mary. Martha. Salammbô, Nana, Sybil, Delfina, Zuleika, Stephanie, Pamela, Cecilia, perhaps Cécile, Celestine, Justine. Not Justine, Justine is completely played out.

"Don't worry."

"I'm not worried. Now come on."

The dialogue shouldn't make too much sense.

The heroine glances at Q. She has already had a couple of dates with him. She likes him, very much, in fact.

"At least consider it, won't you please?"

"I absolutely cannot, what are you thinking of?"

"But if we had lunch together?"

Perhaps she'd glanced at him too often. It was obvious, her fondness for Q. Well, there was nothing for it but to ring up her husband and warn him she wouldn't be home for lunch.

Describe the heroine's husband: blond and short; looks like an underweight *heldentenor*. Not a major character. Relationship · with heroine never brought out clearly. While phoning him she will reminisce about their first meeting; comment on their typical conversations. Then she will tell him she has to have a conference lunch with her publisher and won't be home. In fact not until late, since afterward she has this appointment with a photographer.

My God, what a way to describe me. I'm blond, it's true, but I don't bear the faintest resemblance to a *heldentenor*, underweight or otherwise. Quite apart from the fact Salomé's never set foot inside an opera house and wouldn't know a *heldentenor* from a glockenspiel. And I knew perfectly well what was going on when she rang me up. This so-called publisher she's always dragging out as an excuse is perfectly ludicrous. He wouldn't have time to publish one book a year if he did take her out promptly on the half-hour the way she says. Not that I'm upset or jealous; whenever she's gone I have a chance to do some work—

unless she happens to be in the middle of writing a novel, as now. And then I'm distracted by her notes, which amuse me because I find out everything she's up to. The trouble is, she doesn't do a thing but write books. That phone call to me doesn't give one the faintest idea about her.

Clearly, I shall have to be the precise one and note that this is not a diary. For one thing, the diary/epistolary form is obsolete, and for another, real diaries, i.e. those written for one's own benefit, are meant to be thrown away, not published. This is just my running commentary. When one thinks about it, this could never be a diary; it wouldn't even serve as a letter. Once upon a time, I thought if I ever managed to write to any of my friends I might have photocopies made of choice morsels of this monstrosity of Salomé's and send them off. The point being that her—forgive the word—"novel" would be exposed right now, before she got a chance to publish it. Still, your anonymous reader-at-large compels one to employ a more coherent structure. More imaginary, if you like. I couldn't send this off and have it published. Still, my relationship with Salomé is theatrical anyway, so we'll just have to do it this way, that's all.

If Salomé leaves her notes for this novel lying about, then obviously she intends me to read them. I of course pretend never to have set eyes on them. But from time to time I find hairs planted on a page, or a tiny burglar alarm of two pencil marks aligned one atop the other so Salomé can detect whether the paper underneath has been touched. The amusing little games she plays.

It seems most of the things she writes about happen to

her during the day, but I'm never quite sure. She tends to include confections of her own. The lies she tells to throw smoke up around her absences are obtuse and redundant; I'm convinced she tells them that way to make me aware they're not true. To call a spade a spade, she does it to torture me.

Whenever I check up, I can catch her in lies both to me and to the diary. She's simply a pathological liar, that's all.

The truth does not exist, I will grant you. In the end, Salomé's just a character out of Durrell's *Justine*. If I ever were to let her gain control of me, the way Durrell's Darley did, and try to describe her from only one vantage point, that is my own view of her, I'd necessarily be lying. The only solution is to create several witnesses, several truths.

I've decided to tell it this way, using myself and her view of herself—as she would like to be, that is. ". . . We have to put up with her, like original sin. But to call her a nymphomaniac or to try and Freudianise here . . . takes away all her mythical substance—the only thing she really is. Like all amoral people she verges on the Goddess."*

If I were not to search for her truth among the jottings she leaves around, and if she didn't know I spied on her, and if I weren't a part of the game, we simply would have no relationship at all. It's not as if this game doesn't keep me entertained.

I, just to clear things up straightaway, am Ulrich. I'm completely lacking that drive to succeed that seems to have everybody in thrall these days. Salomé, for instance,

* Lawrence Durrell, *Justine.*

lives on it. "People like Ulrich who, motivated by their character, waver between gentle excess and an equally gentle deficiency come to be defeated . . ."* In any case I detest the idea of being a protagonist. I'm too old, too tired. I'll leave that role to Salomé, or rather the mutation of herself she creates. I'll be useful enough in my role as reflector.

It's a two-game intrigue where, when you think about it, I actually am the hero. Now who the hell is this fellow Q.?

❧ ❧ ❧ ❧ ❧ ❧ ❧ ❧ ❧ ❧ ❧

At lunch they weren't alone. A girlfriend of Q.'s was there unexpectedly.

Damn these names anyway. Not one comes to mind.

Great violet eyes, this friend of Q.'s; she talked on and on.

"You haven't said a thing to me."

"It's not as if I've had the chance."

"You do now."

"What about?"

Q. touched her hand under the table. "What we were talking about before." Then he takes hold of her hand under the table. Lovely, these forbidden things. She grazes his jacket with her elbow. Daring.

"Ah, yes."

The heroine finished her steak and placed her knife on

* Robert Musil, *The Man without Qualities.*

the plate. She took Q.'s hand and squeezed it. Under the table.

"Perhaps it wouldn't be such a bad idea to talk about it for a while."

"About that matter?"

"Perhaps after lunch, if you have time."

"Certainly I've got time. Shall we have coffee somewhere?"

Instead they went to Q.'s hotel, where they had trouble getting up to his room. But Q. passed her off as his wife, who'd arrived after losing her cases in transit; they'd just been married. "No luggage?" the porter asked for the third time. Q. obviously was expert at maneuvering these things, something so few men do properly, organizing love.

Making love to Q. Love-making with Q. In fact, screwing Q.

Meanwhile they've begun calling each other by their first names.

The heroine undresses while Q. watches. "How lovely it'll be to make love to you." The idiotic things Q. said. Q. is unusual, a character more or less. Mark, Luke, Jason, Apollo: that's not bad. Albert?

What was Q. thinking of? Windows closed, all the lights on: it was like being inside a gymnasium.

Q. is twenty-nine, maybe a little older. He has abstract and very mysterious ways of conversing. He runs around Europe dressed most peculiarly. You know what I can't abide? The way other people are always taking your picture. Q., will you please be serious. I am, I'm perfectly serious. Now it's my turn to take a picture of you. Look how beautiful you are, all that white skin. He has a

Polaroid. He likes making love. He keeps his eyes closed. Nearly everybody makes love alone, it's a projection of oneself that way, a kind of narcissism. You really think so? A clinical fact, I assure you. I must tell you how crazy I am about your face. She likes Q.'s kissing inside her mouth. I must tell you how crazy I am about the way you kiss. More? Shall we do it all over again?

Q.'s the kind who wouldn't run after just any girl. Unusual for him that he took her to bed right off. But after all, she's over twenty-one.

She's much too hurried with her characters, she doesn't give them time to gel, she doesn't give a damn about any of them. Her method of writing is most unorthodox. The first book was a bestseller and a bloody nuisance. In fact it was sheer hell: the phone ringing incessantly, reporters and new friends hanging around, invitations pouring in. I found it impossible to finish anything I started. I've been two years now on this damned Milton translation and I've completely lost the enthusiasm I originally had for putting the entirety of *Paradise Lost* into readable Italian. My whole approach now seems wrong. The explanation is, very simply, that Salomé emasculates me with all these books she turns out. I'm the first one to admit that. She used to snarl at me over the breakfast table: "You don't suppose you're the only living being who can write a book, do you?" Very smug. That was when she was keeping her first novel under lock and key.

My publisher is still waiting for me to turn in the Milton. I'll have to put him off with a promise to send some new poems of my own.

When they gave me a prize for my book of poetry, Salomé was wild with jealousy. Then MGM bought those two wretched novels of hers, made two monstrous films out of them, and she consoled herself buying one white Porsche.

It would rather please me if Salomé were to have a child. At least she'd keep quiet for a few months. It might force her to write something decent instead of these diaries disguised as novels.

Now who is this bloody Q.? Maybe I don't know him, but she says she had already met him a couple of times, so possibly I've seen him too. It boggles the mind, all these men who take her to bed. Even worse is the quantity of lies she tells: "I'm going to tea with my aunt." As if she had an aunt. As if she were the type to mingle with the relations. Pseudo-errands all afternoon, a meeting with her editor, dinner with her American publisher, the Swedish publisher too: "My publisher says I must, otherwise I shouldn't bother at all." An emergency two-hour meeting with the publisher's art director about a jacket design. I'd much rather she didn't invent these things. A simple "I'm going out now," and that would be that. After all, I read what she does a couple of days later anyway. Salomé knows I read her notes: she leaves them open at the right place, these manuscripts. The curious thing is that I'm fascinated. Her relationship with me interests her only insofar as I am The Spectator.

Really. A *heldentenor.* What could be further from the truth?

All this business with Q., though, might actually be true. But it's entirely possible it's imaginary. Just to torment me. Sometimes I've accidentally discovered that her most graphically described sex scenes with the most obvious characters, the ones you recognize instantly, have never happened. She's not beneath describing a sexual encounter with de Gaulle—places, dates, conversations— and she's never even been introduced to the General, I'm sure of it.

Just for my benefit, all this: so it must mean that she loves me, in her way. She wants to hold me, to entertain me with her literary puzzles, that's obvious. Part of the game lies in the fact that Salomé knows I try to distinguish which of her characters and episodes are invented and which are real.

Unless everything she writes is fiction.

Here I will write about Salomé, using her notebook. It seems to be the only way. "Put a novelist into the novel. He justifies æsthetic generalizations. . . . He also justifies experiment." Even more apt: "But why draw the line at one novelist inside your novel? Why not a second inside his? And a third inside the novel of the second? And so on to infinity . . ."*

Salomé used to be different. Who knows why she married me.—Fascinated, I suppose, with the idea that I

* Aldous Huxley, *Point Counter Point.*

was a writer and actually serious about it. The aphrodisiac of the printed page. That's what she used to say. My taking a month to work over a single poem. Now the same thing drives her mad. I like the way she dresses, Salomé, that is. Peacock feathers on her hats and skirts, black dresses down to her ankles, ornately embroidered cloaks, black lace blouses that disintegrate and shed all over her other expensive things. Her necklines are always, well, plunging.

Whenever she comes into a room, she's so tall she unnerves me. Her wide, fleshy lips painted small. I sometimes ask myself if I love her in spite of everything, this wife of mine. And what ties us together, apart from our maid and these literary lies.

One day she'll leave me. As it is now, she has more money than I do, more friends, whom she thinks are better than mine (she's quite wrong). And I won't know until too late because she won't describe the desertion until a couple of days afterward: "And she said to her husband, 'Dear, don't you think life would be simpler if we separated?' —Her husband looked at her with that air of underweight *heldentenor*. 'It will make me unhappy, my dear.'"

Then as usual I won't be described at all. The devil knows whom she'll leave me for. The hell of it is that I really do care for Salomé, even if she does disappear for days on end, lie, and show up only to write these journals that paralyze my days. It's hard to believe I used to be able to work ten hours a day.

This is a form of masochism. But what else is Salomé capable of inspiring, with that face all jutting angles?

After making love with Q., the heroine took a shower and carefully put on her face. She made up her face. Made up her face is better. Put on her face is such a vulgar expression. Put on, never; perhaps make up. Put on her makeup. Painted herself up, too contrived. Unless I say carefully applied her eyeliner and lipstick.

"Why are you getting all got-up?" (Q.)

"Certainly not for you."

"I like it anyhow."

"Does it change me much?" (Heroine)

"No, no. But it does look smashing. In fact you look grand."

"I'm having some pictures taken. A famous photographer."

"Are you photogenic?"

"So-so."

"And did you like it?"

"What?"

"The things we did together."

"Of course I did."

They go into another clinch. Q. still tasted of her all over, and in spite of her shower the heroine still tasted of Q.

"Now let me alone, I'm trying to fix my hair."

"All right, I'll let you alone."

Watch out for this sort of dialogue, it gets boring very fast.

"Are you really going to a photographer's?"

"Of course I am. You don't think I'd tell you lies?"

"You told your husband so many over the phone."

"My husband likes it that way."

"Who's taking your picture?"

"Donny Golucky."

"It seems he's extraordinary."

"Photographers are all alike. The best ones cheat."

"What do you mean?"

"The good ones give you something to do, they talk all the time, and they all wind up making pictures of themselves. One of them took about twenty rolls of me: every single frame looked exactly like his wife. Another made me the ideal he had in his mind's eye, he said, absolutely pure. I came out looking like a Sacred Heart boarder."

Q. took her in his arms. "You really amuse me, you know." Mathô (the slave), Nérac, Dorian (rather common now, after a soubrette called herself that), Egon, Alistair? Hello, who's calling please? Egon calling. Egon will do.

❖❖❖❖❖❖❖❖❖❖

I'm astonished: she actually did go to the photographer's. I never would have believed it. So she sometimes even tells the truth. Naturally she would let Q. (Egon, now) think I enjoy hearing her lies, but maybe that was only her way of dragging me into the novel. Perhaps Salomé wants to get back at me for something I've done. I know one thing about me that irritates her enormously: that I take my writing seriously. She tells me it's sour grapes. Brooding for hours over a single word; translating poetry —what makes me do it? None of it brings in any money, not even enough to buy groceries. That's it: she despises me because I earn so little money. I recall, however, that it made her euphoric, my publishing those three poems dedicated to her. Too abstract for me, she said; nobody's going to read them, but in any case it was sweet of you to dedicate them to me. And they're full of the cleverest words, none of which I understand, though.

We still make love occasionally. Not that it amuses Salomé. Salomé goes to bed with everybody, or nearly everybody—out of insecurity, like all women. Perhaps I'm incapable of entertaining her, I don't give her enough. But I have changed her; before we were married she was much worse.

This last bit of hers is passable. The dialogue is not bad; she has written so much that she's finally got the hang of it. She will spend hours at her desk; then she'll tell a couple of lies, make a phone call, and run out. The upshot is that I never see her. Some nights she disappears with her friends and doesn't turn up for a week. I never go along because I can't stand her friends: film people, actors, directors—or, even worse, theatre people. And that raft of photographers and reporters.

A *heldentenor*. Now what can she mean by that, My husband has the air of an underweight *heldentenor?* She must have picked the phrase up someplace. She has an infallible ear. She makes it a point never to read anything; two or three pages of a book and she knows what's going to happen. Or she skims a review and pretends to have read the book. It's my job to write, she says, not to read. How would I find the time?

The doorbell's just rung. Ah, the maid's getting it. Madame is not at home. True, Salomé went off for the weekend . . . with her publisher again. Come along if you want, said she, but that actor will be there. . . . In other words, she told me to stay home. Maybe she's with Q. The delivery was a telegram for Salomé: CAN'T MEET YOU BUSINESS APPOINTMENTS LOVE EGON. So at least we know she's not with him. Let's hope she uses "Q." or something in the book, and not his real name.

Justine before the multiple mirrors: "Look! five different pictures of the same subject. Now if I wrote I would try for a multi-dimensional effect in character, a sort of prism-sightedness. Why should not people show more than one profile at a time?"*

❧ ❧ ❧ ❧ ❧ ❧ ❧ ❧ ❧ ❧ ❧

"My baggage will be along later," the heroine assured the hotel porter. She went out into the rain to hail a cab. Egon will tell the porter he had a fight with his wife and she won't be back. He's expert at lying too, but without the subtle give-and-take of a game. Unilateral lying, not very

* Durrell, *Op. cit.*

funny. To Q., there were only two sins: murder and kick-
ing paralytic old ladies. Everything else was cricket. Actually he had a point. She liked this Q. (Egon), the
heroine thought. She paid the cabbie and, still in a
trance of lovemaking, climbed the stairs to Golucky's
place. The receptionist asked her to wait. Pictures everywhere, extremely beautiful, blond, enormous-eyed, enor-
mous-mouthed women. Follow me please. Mr. Golucky
will be with you in a moment.

They went up to the studio: a cavernous room, reflectors
and lights of all sorts, rolls of colored poster paper
crammed into the corners, umbrellas covered with tinfoil,
machines, automatic shutters, electric and manual fans,
cameras, tripods, sawhorses. The heroine inspected herself in a mirror. Luckily her husband had turned down the
weekend invitation, so she'd go see E. that night. Then
she'd move on to spend the weekend at Esmé Aitken-
Percy's. Possibly the loveliest house she'd ever seen; a bit
dank, to be sure, but never mind that. Labyrinths of rooms
and completely enthralling hallways. Golucky came in.
"You seem tolerably good-looking," he said, squaring her
off. "Shame your forehead isn't half an inch higher and
your face is so small. Of course your mouth is a disaster.
We'll try to elongate it with the lights. Have to use lenses
too. That black lace. Utterly destroys the tone of your com-
plexion. None too good to start with. Get out of it immediately."

"What do I put on then?"

"Anything, anything, wrap a towel around your bra."

"Good lord, I'm a writer. I can't have myself photographed like a common cover girl."

"Who says all women writers have to look like hags in their pictures."

The heroine does as she is told. Let's try calling her Davina. Davina obeyed. "What are they paying you to take my picture?"

"I'm not at liberty to say. But I don't work unless I can make three million a week. When I was young, I'm thirty now dammit all, I got it into my head that I had to make at least three million a week. Two or three publicity campaigns, the rounds with a model, a junket off to Persia with her for some location shots. Total dog's life, you know. Don't let's dwell on it. But you come out with valuable experience. Now I've bought myself a haberdashery. My friends warned me not to, said it was doomed right off. If it bombs, what's it to me? I close up shop, I told them, and forget it. In fact it's doing terrifically well. Making loot hand over fist. You've just got to get your foot in the door. Once one thing's a hit, everything else trots right along behind. And if it doesn't work out the first time, try try again. That's my philosophy."

"And where's this shop of yours?"

"What! You don't know it? Donny's? Surely you've been there a thousand times, everybody goes there. I've also got a construction company. When I was redoing my apartment I couldn't keep my workmen, so instead of going to a builder I hired my own, stole the carpenter, electrician, bricklayer away and kept them for myself. The apartment ended up costing me nothing. And my little company is doing just fine. If there's work, they earn, if not, they don't get paid. That's how labor should be handled these days. Sit still and don't move your mouth.

I'll put some glycerine on. Angelo. The silk brush. Angelo. What the fuck are you doing, Angelo? Where are those goddam lights?"

He surrounded her with lights and cameras.

"I'm nasty to Angelo but actually he's a genius, almost as good as I am. Your hair's too short. People have told me a few things about you. I, on the other hand, am divorced. I've got two kids. I was married at nineteen, can you imagine. Some day you ought to come by my apartment, it's really swish. It's in via Condotti. There's a garage downstairs where I keep my Ferrari. Did you know I had a Ferrari? My very own, just to putter around in. It's not a bad life. In the morning a cabbie brings me breakfast from the Ritz if I haven't time to go myself. What about putting a wig on you, sweetheart?"

"No, then I shouldn't look myself."

"Angelo. Get that other fellow What's-his-face in here. You haven't done a bloody fucking thing all day long. I'm doing all the work myself. I don't underpay you for nothing. Bring that wind machine over here, let's get a little of that hair on your face. Out of sight, man. Now dear, let's not drift off into trances. Eyes into the camera."

He ran through a Rolleicord first, then an assortment of Japanese cameras, then a Leica, then a Rolleiflex.

"I've got twenty or so. You can't work with less. All these parvenu camera bugs who think they know everything."

"It must be a fascinating job."

"In fact it's a bloody bore. A few years at it and I've got all the money I'll ever need. Then I've bought this little village a few miles from Biarritz and I'm having it restored. I'll make a fortune off it. I've designed some jewelry and some plasticene furniture. That's gone over so well I've decided to manufacture it myself. I'm thinking about a ski resort in the Alps, a lot of ghastly little bungalows to sell to your typical halfwit middle-class-rich family."

Davina scratched her head.

"Would you mind sitting still. Your mouth is really atrocious. Angelo. More glycerine. Take off that towel, let's see some more skin. Now let's put you behind the paper. Move it, slaves, get to work."

His two assistants wheeled out a roll of black paper from one of the corners and attached it to the ceiling.

"Please sit behind it."

Donny Golucky pulled out a lethal-looking switchblade and began to make slashes in the sheet of paper. First a square that revealed Davina's face. Then holes that filtered through light from the spots behind Donny.

"You look like a sculptor."

"Exactly. I'm sculpting the light on your face with knife strokes. Nothing comes through that I don't want. This way I can shape your face and try to improve it."

"But there's nothing wrong with my face."

"What do you know about faces."

"Well—"

"It's the most beautiful thing in the world."

"What, my face?"

"No. Modeling with light."

Another slash. The light bathed Davina and the cameras began to chatter.

At least she had the good taste not to go to bed with that one; though perhaps the reason she left out the vital detail is that it's perfectly obvious who this Golucky is. The other day Salomé came up to me and told me point-blank that she loved me. God knows what provoked that. "I wish you'd change a little, dear. You're withdrawing," she informed me. "Look how you keep yourself occupied— translating, writing those dear little poems I don't understand. People laugh at you and won't invite us out any more." I told her I didn't give a damn if people don't invite us out any more. It's not that they won't invite *me* out, they know I won't go anyway. I told her the truth, that people talk about her all the time, and it's because of those little tales she tells in her books. "They're none too obscure, you know, in fact you go beyond the call of duty making them explicit." "Well dear, what *are* people saying?" "They gossip." "Don't tell me you care." —In other words, we quarreled, something I never do because it makes me very high-strung and I can't sleep. I detest raising my voice, I detest scenes, and since Salomé isn't capable of discussing anything any other way, I retreat to my room and read the papers the minute I see one coming. She upsets my stomach, with all that deafening shouting. Salomé says I'm a coward and perhaps I am. But I had so many scenes at home when I was little; my father and mother did nothing but fight. It made them happy, they even loved one another.

The scene at the photographer's isn't bad. Salomé's quite good at creating a character in a few pages, if she feels like it. What she doesn't make up, she simply incorporates intact from real life. One day I'll write a book about Salomé, nothing like this though. This one is about me and how Salomé views herself. I will describe her realistically. No, that's out of the question. "If reality were simply statement of fact, then a kind of cinematographic film would certainly suffice, and 'style' and 'literature' departing from their barest factual substance would be superfluous artifices."*

❦❦❦❦❦❦❦❦❦❦❦

That night Davina did not go home. She rang her husband to say she couldn't and arrived at E.'s in the late afternoon, his house glowing in the sun and the flowers tinted by the sunset. Inside the house there were clouds of narcissus and white orchids; succulent flowers, they looked a bit like E.

Perhaps we should change this name Davina. Cecilia. "Cécile" doesn't sound right at all. Perhaps Candida wouldn't be bad. Or Samantha. But the heroine's name ought to begin with a vowel too. That way I'll get some nice assonances going. A. ate with E. E. eased out of A.'s

* Marcel Proust, *Le Temps retrouvé.*

arms, and so forth. But then Eloise suits her to a tee. Drop the aitch and dieresis from Peter Abelard's lady friend. It's old-fashioned enough and unquestionably conveys the aura of a heroine. Let's hope people don't start thinking about that American novelty book about the little girl.

Before this scene, describe how Eloise first met E.

The encounter should be described in detail and beautifully poetic to read. Repeat every word of their first conversation, carefully designed to be utterly pleasing. No personal questions, just generalities.

"I can't abide places like this." (E.)

"Why come here then?" (Eloise)

"I don't often. But if you've got houses, you know, you're obliged to look after them from time to time, to make sure the servants haven't turned them into hotels. Once every two years is often enough."

"It's a shame the people who frequent this place are so monstrous. And so many of them."

"Actually over at my place it's rather quiet."

They're at dinner with some people. Eloise is sitting at E.'s right. Dismal restaurant, the hanging-oil-lamp and lit-fireplace variety, with fake hams everywhere.

Eloise: "What shall we have for a second course? Shall we trust the scampi? They're such a mess to eat."

"Go ahead and eat them any way you like."

"Are you staying long?"

"Not really. I'm traveling round. I have to get back on the train as soon as I've been in a place for a few hours."

"I abhor trains."

"How sad."

"What do you mean, how sad?"

"It upsets me you don't like something I love. Up till now, we agreed about everything."

"If we liked all the same things, we wouldn't have a thing to say to one another. I for example live on the phone." (Eloise)

"So do I." (E.)

"I adore chocolate." (Eloise)

"Can't abide it." (E.)

"How sad." (Eloise)

"Now you stop saying how sad." (E.)

"Oysters." (Eloise)

"Adore them." (E.)

"Power." (Eloise)

"Me too." (E.)

"You've just let out a well-kept state secret, sir." (Eloise)

"I like you." (E.)

"Me, too." (Eloise)

"What, you like yourself?" (E.)

"No, of course I meant you. Very much." (Eloise)

"Then why don't you call me by my first name?" (E.)

"You intimidate me too much. You're so important." (Eloise)

"Don't be such a little hypocrite, it excites you that I'm important." (E.)

"Quite so."

"Actually it's a bore. You're always moving round, you can't really settle in anywhere. A group like ours can't stay in one place; you have to think how to make a journey fast and comfortably every waking moment."

"You're talking to yourself now."

"Not at all, I'm just preparing you."

"Were you preparing me? Now aren't you considerate."

After the restaurant, though, more impersonal chatter. Much faster, jumbled banter. Social gossip.

"I tell you, she's a cretin."

"Nothing new, she's famous for it, everybody knows."

"She simply takes aim and fires."

"Not at all, I've never known her to take aim. It's a mystery what motivates her."

"Have you ever met her?"

"God no. Never."

"Quite right not to have met her."

"But the way she dresses. Always in the glossies looking like a gypsy."

"The entire family is insane."

"Then they pretend to be aristocrats."

"When the truth is they'll even go to bed for money. Impossible people."

"Cretins, you're perfectly right."

"Notorious."

Eventually Eloise and E. make love. They both know they will (so should the reader), but they go on chattering for a couple of hours. E. is a lion in bed. Eloise has never experienced anybody who makes love like him. He wakes her up in the morning as soon as he's shaved and showered. He makes love to her again, several times, then they leave together.

Describe the two of them alone together for a couple of days. E. should be the hero of this story (providing Q.-Egon doesn't take over). E. will reappear from time to time. He isn't part of Eloise's life, he just comes and goes. Since he isn't like any other man, he's difficult to explain and I won't describe him in much detail. I'll only say he's handsome. The rest will come from the conversations. He doesn't have a relationship with Eloise because E. is not the kind for relationships. That's the point of him: emphasize it. At twenty-five-page intervals, phone calls. "And how is Miss Eloise today? Where in hell have you been? Why haven't you rung up before? What are you doing in that squalid city? Whom are you seeing? Are you coming over tonight? —No, tomorrow.— I'll ship you back tomorrow night or the day after. You'll never guess who I saw, that imbecile friend of yours. A perfect moron and you know it. What do you mean? I am not. I'm still here, as always vegetating. What else are you up to? Never mind, save it, you're coming tonight."

Those phone calls made Eloise a bit nervous. First, the secretary answering over the wire. Then his voice, his wild outbursts, his stories. Perhaps make more of these phone calls. Fewer but longer? Or more but shorter? Always E.'s voice alone.

At E.'s country house.

Naturally E. hasn't arrived yet. Eloise walked around the swimming pool and explored the garden. The hedges were infested with flowers.

A series of bells, phones, warnings: E. has passed the gatehouse. She heard the car but couldn't make it out through the shrubbery. Flowers clogging the view. There he was, so handsome, coming down the slope toward her. In slow motion. Eloise got up, intending to meet him halfway. But she was so taken with the tableau of his approach, she wanted to savor it, memorize it. Too late: there he was, beside her.

"How are you?" A kiss on the cheek.

"Well, as always. How handsome you look." Touch him, all over. His face first.

"Actually I'm done in." Take his hands comfortingly. It was the first time he'd admitted any such thing. Fatigue, debility are afflictions of the ordinary human being. E. was not even a human being, much less ordinary. Which he knew, more or less. Maybe he only suspected it.

"How lovely it is here."

They had lunch. Describe the food and table setting. Also the way the courses are served. Also the stories E. tells, so different from typical weekend chatter where nobody says anything. This section ought to be eight or so pages long.

As if one didn't know right off who this E. is: everybody will. She should be more circumspect in these descriptions, really. I ought to take advantage of her being gone and try to forge on with the translating. But here I am, throwing away this free time as usual. Nothing's working: I've too many notes and versions and it would take more energy than I have right now to sort them out. The ignominious truth is, I would rather work on this book. Salomé was saying that the Milton was perfectly all right in its present state. She's a fine one: she's never so much as glanced at it. What would help me would be an editor ringing me up every five minutes to find out how I was coming along. Just somebody to *care*, damn it. But what difference could it make to any of them. My books aren't the kind that coin money the way Salomé's seem to.

Perhaps I was different once. I'm 53 now. If I were to describe myself, I'd have to fall back on Musil again. "He was happy, never seeing anyone. People were hard to take."* Once in a while I think about death and how close I am to it. I'll die soon. If I stay at home all the time like this, I shall certainly die of lack of oxygen.

I can see this book already in print; the problem is writing it. It's out of the question to finish this book in less than two years. The other novel took five years of sheer torture. But this book about Salomé is going to be something else. Perhaps the protagonist will end up being the conjugal game. And without the husband as accomplice, a man without qualities like me who plays along with it, the heroine wouldn't stand up. But of course she really isn't a heroine anyway.

☙ ☙ ☙ ☙ ☙ ☙ ☙ ☙ ☙ ☙ ☙

Scene: Paduan plane. A mixture of heavy mist and industrial smoke.

The guests at Atalanta Alighieri-Estense's (age forty)

* Musil, *op. cit.*

and her husband Tristano's (about fifty; passive, taciturn, with a wife like Atalanta he has no choice) are:

Angela, friend and relative of Atalanta's. Spinster in her fifties, knows everything about flowers and dogs, complains of imaginary ills.

Xenia, now in her eighties, Atalanta's old nanny-governess.

Benito Ercolini, elegant, famous, titled, president of many committees, not a genius.

Brief appearance of *Edward,* his friend, very young.

Erode Mangiagalli, banker, Sicilian, political personality, president of more committees than Ercolini, also a Senator. Emaciated, cadaverous, completely hairless, and powerful.

Sandrino Bosanquette, opera designer, many times booed at La Scala, the Metropolitan (not at Covent Garden Opera House, that is, The Royal Opera House, as the English public is so polite and genteel), now Mangiagalli's mistress, or rather lover. Influential in pseudo-intellectual, pseudo-social circles; always in a foul mood. Probably has colitis.

Egon (Q.).

Ismene, Egon's wife.

Eloise, heroine.

Atalanta's house is superb. A park, waterfalls, marble statues all around. A castle inside and out: a pastiche of sixteenth-century and baroque architecture with Palladian touches here and there. Colonnades, atriums, vestibules. Capitals. Inside, sublime pictures and autograph furniture. Describe it more clearly.

Atalanta went with Eloise up. (That's nice iambic pen-

tameter; better not ruin the effect with "to her room."–
Good lord, what am I thinking of? This is prose.) Atalanta
went with Eloise up to her room.

"You must remember to use this staircase, my dear.
Don't be afraid of the dogs. They make a lot of noise, but
they're just letting off steam, showing their high spirits.
All bark, as they say. There must be a hundred of them
around the house. Xenia's always attacking me about the
mistakes, you know, the mongrels. She's such a snob. I
hope you'll be all right here. This is your bath. Then you're
sharing a sitting room with Egon and his wife Ismene,
who haven't arrived yet, as usual. They sleep in the other
two rooms and have a bath of their own. I didn't put you
in the west wing because last Sunday a canopy fell in on
my sister-in-law. She took offense and said it was a joke
in very poor taste. As if it were the sort of joke I play all
the time. It was Tristano's idea, not mine. Have you seen
E. recently? Is he all right? He *is* magnificent. So nice,
and it's all genuine. Top drawer. We never see him any
more. Tea's served at five, dinner at eight. It varies somewhat, of course. Erode Mangiagalli will be here too. You
know him, don't you? But he's marvelous. Hideous to look
at, I'll grant you, but exquisite inside. Of course he's got
a finger in every pie in this country. Extremely important.
All you have to do is drop a hint and he can arrange anything. He's gotten together everything from tontines to
charitable funds. Of course Sandrino is coming. He's a
perfect bitch, but so entertaining. I'm positive he'll despise
you. He's allergic to heterosexuals. He says he likes me
not as a friend but because I'm very mannish. One of his
more tactful statements. But poor thing, he can't help
making people suffer; and then people who suffer are such

bores. But I'll tell you one thing, people who make other
people suffer tend to have bad breath. All a question of
digestion. Who else? Oh, Benito Ercolini, who always
lends us his box at La Scala. He's no genius, to be sure,
but he's still good looking. Be careful not to criticize anything in front of him; he's president of everything and it
makes him furious to hear bad things about any of it.
Even the newspapers, mind you, so watch out. Then
there's Angela and Xenia, who don't count. Angela's been
a friend forever, we insult each other twenty-four hours
a day. She's also related to me. Tristano despises her, but
I love her dearly. Come on, I'll take you out to see the
garden." They descended the grand staircase.

*Legs first. Aristoc talks the language of legs. Life's fine, this
is 1969! Courtelle Year! How to tell a woman from a man.
Life has some marvelous things in store for you. Don't
"man-talk" me! It scintillates! It sparkles! It makes you
look alive! Try a Senator, darling, they're cool! Mrs. B. is
giving a small ball for her daughter on the 14th of De-
cember.*

Veronese frescoes.

"This looks to be a Rubens, but if you ask me, it's a
forgery. It's too pretty to be real. Look, here's Angela.
Where are you off to, dear? She's always stuffing her face
with chocolates behind my back. Why don't you come
with us into the garden?"

Atalanta: tall, short-cropped hair around her pointy
face. In a way she looks like the heroine. Long pants and
packs of hounds trailing after her.

"This is my darling, my wee babe. He's the son of that

sow Evelyn who wanders round screwing indiscriminately and dropping illegitimate monsters like him. She's about to have another litter; doubtless she'll have six, which is her usual performance. And ruin my weekend. Then Charlie the setter scratched his eye last night and the vet says he'll probably lose it. That's the end of those blue ribbons. I was up all last night with the eyedropper holding Charlie's paw, poor Charlie. Angela, look at that *Cinararia aequitribola* and the *Cymbalaria pallida* I had my cousin send me. When it arrived at the greenhouse I was sure it was all dead. Now look where it's got to, it's invaded the mortar."

"You ought to try out *Tunica saxifraga* over by those rocks. I've got some *Silene acaulis,* but it tends to get out of hand too."

"Angela, you make the damnedest messes in your garden. That *Pedalineae* you've got, I must admit, is very nice. Do put some in a box with some earth and mail it to me. I think I'll plant some *Polygonum cuspidatum.* What's your opinion, Eloise?"

"It'll be grand, I'm sure."

"Angela's always picking on me because I've got *Prunus biferium* instead of the *pennsylvanica.* I'm positive they're identical. It doesn't interest me in the slightest, this quibbling about which species is the rarest. Angela takes the most ghoulish delight in torturing me. Well, well, look who's turned up at long last. Sandrino, and my dear Mangiagalli. How are you? Did you have a pleasant journey? This is our Eloise, I told you about her. You already know Angela, don't you? For years, I should imagine, since she's been around for the past century."

"How are you?" Erode Mangiagalli said to Angela.

"Not very well, you know, this arthritis is always with

me, but the doctor's promised to come today. Of course you can't get near the phone in this house, what with Atalanta continually ringing up every vet in a ten-mile radius; one could bleed to death. Besides that, I've got this dreary ache in my thigh."

"Can't you hear the violins in the background? Don't encourage her, Erode, she's healthy as an ox."

"How are you?" (Eloise to Sandrino Bosanquette)

"Quite satisfactory, thank you," he replied, frigid.

Mangiagalli, on the other hand, took a liking to Eloise. He was the ugliest man she'd ever set eyes on. Thin as a camel after a six-month caravan, convex-concave spine, he looked more like a sea creature than a Senator—an effect enhanced by the fact that all his visible flesh was hairless as the palms of his hands; and it was the color of mushrooms, except for traceries of blue veins here and there. But he had the fascination of power, so Eloise forgave him his looks.

"You write very well," Mangiagalli said. "Congratulations."

"I'm sure he's never read a book in his life, much less one of yours," said Atalanta, heading back toward the house. "But he is terrific. He plays everything by ear. Money for a literary prize, or funds for a repertory company, just like that. Imagine how much time it saves him. And it doesn't upset anybody. He's a marvelous man. Everybody says he's corrupt, but I don't care. Anyhow, I can't think of a soul who isn't, can you?"

Egon and Ismene arrived very late. Egon was always late. One of those people who catch the right train or plane by dumb luck, who arrive an hour late for dinner. They all took tea in the blue room.

"She's a rutting sow, I can't understand why Atalanta lets her inside the house," Xenia was growling. "You can tell right off, not an ounce of breeding, she behaves barbarically. That mangy skin, and her tail's half bald."

"Just like dear Evelyn. I don't know what causes it. But look at Annie, though, hasn't she a magnificent profile? Not a brain inside that flawless skull, but she's very sweet. She's always pregnant and curled up in front of the fire, never doing anybody any harm. I don't know why you continually pick on her."

"She'll couple with anything. You can't stop her, she's a nymphomaniac. When she's not in heat, she finds some way to deceive the males. She's done nothing but fill this house up with mongrels covered with those obscene spots of mange."

Angela was telling Benito Ercolini about her aches and pains. She didn't know what else to say to him.

Alchimenes, Tigridia, Zephyrantes candida, Muscari, Gloxinia, Fritillaria, Chionodoxa, Agapanthus, Allium moly, Ornithogalum.

Q. was sitting next to Eloise. "Later tonight I'll join you in bed."

"Will you please keep your voice down." (Eloise)

"If I keep my voice down, they'll all know we're up to something. The thing to do is talk loud, then nobody will suspect I'm saying these things to you over a cup of tea with my wife in the same room."

"In any case, it's out of the question." (Eloise)

"I've had a look, you know. We're in the same suite. When they're all asleep, I'll come round." (Q.-Egon)

"But Ismene will know." (Eloise)

"Nonsense, she sleeps like a corpse." (Q.)

"And who's going to wake you up so you can scamper back to your room, the chambermaid?" (Eloise)

"I wake up early. Not very though, around ten."

"Who's this that's threatening to get up at ten?" Atalanta asked, bristling. "Look here, breakfast is served in bed or the yellow dining room until nine. After that, you're all welcome to starve."

"I never have breakfast, I might as well warn you now."

"Well, I do," said Xenia. "I'd abolish all meals but breakfast and tea. I adore cakes and all those divine marmalades, all colors and flavors. Not to mention fresh brioches and croissants, homemade ones. Steaks couldn't matter less to me."

"It's perfect for you to feel that way. After all, you're a nanny."

"That's why Xenia's always sick."

"She's not sick. She's only a hypochondriac," Angela asserted. "There's nothing seriously wrong with her, the way there is with me."

Ismene was almost asleep. "I must go and have a nap."

"If Evelyn drops her litter tonight, don't expect me at dinner."

"It won't do not to have the lady of the house at table," Tristano said.

"Be good enough to mind your own business, will you. Besides, with me gone you'll come out even, since we've got two women too many. Actually no, just one, because Xenia eats by herself. Anyhow, she doesn't count."

"Now don't start insulting me just because I'm old."

"Old, good heavens, you're a mere babe," Tristano said laughing, all aglow for having said something.

Ercolini had moved over to sit by Bosanquette, who

enjoyed it. Mangiagalli was with Eloise. Egon had disappeared with his wife.

"We need young blood like you writing." (Erode Mangiagalli)

"It must be marvelous to be able to decide things. I envy you." (Eloise)

"But if you only knew how much work there is. One thing gives rise to a thousand others, not a minute of peace. Phone calls, appointments, Senate, Cabinet meetings, round table discussions, people to see. At night I ought to rest, relax, but the social life is enervating, incessant."

For Mangiagalli this was victory, to be accepted in spite of his ugliness. It was nearly impossible to open the newspaper without coming across the man's image:

I've only room to name a few of the people present: Daphne Lady Poohe, Madame Erich von Schultess-Rechbergson, Principessa Alexa Roverelli, the Pope's niece, charming in her very witty geranium chapeau. Also Lady Sarahjane Hope-Morrow, Lady Porchester, the lovely dress-designer, the Principessa Solleone-Paceli, the annulment of whose marriage to Prince Solleone-Paceli, the nephew of the Pope, was announced last week. Also the great-grandmother of the hostess, Contessa Marietta Bagliotti-Ghiotti, splendid in her pink lace gown. Niall Philpott, the celebrated writer, and his companion Varicella Malati; Elvilda Anystruther-Gough-Calthorpe and her splendid daughter Stephanie who's just returned from Nassau where she spent the season; she has announced that she will take up acting, hoping to star in the new Fellini film. The Sicilian Minister, Erode Mangiagalli, proposed the toast. Sandrino Bosanquette was accompanied by a friend from Paris, Mme Borel de Biche.

Three days disgracefully wasted fixing dates for the 1970 Red Cross Ball. In spite of the Socialist Party being back in power, the season is proceeding splendidly. I've already got up nearly fifty balls and cocktail parties for next year. Among these, one for Sandrino Bosanquette, creator of the interesting sets for "Il ballo in maschera." The lovely Miss Zedelia Crowther will entertain a hundred guests at an intimate ball to start off the season.

Absolutely brilliant as usual, Signor Mangiagalli was the life of the party with his witty remarks.

In a toast, the Sicilian Minister, Erode Mangiagalli, committed a considerable sum to the company for expansion and improvements.

The evening would not have been nearly so pleasant if the presence of Erode Mangiagalli had not refreshed it with the promise of several million lire for next year's exposition.

"There are two things I'd like to ask you." (Eloise)

"Speak up, speak up. I can do anything. I've got swarms of industrialists panting to donate billions to anything. To get in my good graces and, of course, to help with taxes. Also to be invited around. Why not, they've done nothing but work their fingers to the bone all their lives. Beautiful houses, ancient wives, grown-up children: what else is there to go after? Social recognition. Ask, ask for anything you like. I tell you, they hang around clamoring for a chance to give."

"For instance, I know a group of very talented young people, a repertory company. Of course they've no money and since they tend to do experimental theatre, they don't stand a chance of making any. That's the sort of thing I feel is worth patronizing."

"But my dear, nothing could be simpler. We'll just get together a couple of big names, a few titles, Sandrino, a few famous philanthropists, and I guarantee forty million in a few weeks. I'm serious, do tell your young people to go ahead and do anything they like. What's the second thing? If it's something like this, don't give it a second thought, it's no trouble at all."

"Actually, the other thing is my husband, who's a good writer, very serious, very dedicated. He just needs a little recognition. You know the type, hunched over his desk for forty years. A prize, a political appointment. His sort is very useful on committees . . ."

"You're married? I had no idea. But of course, this is no problem either."

❖❖❖❖❖❖❖❖❖❖

That explains the Minister's ringing me up. What on earth was Salomé thinking of, putting him up to it? Here I've actually gone and accepted the invitation and I'll have to go by myself, since as usual Salomé's nowhere to be found. A flower of deceit, that man, a corrupt philistine is precisely what he is. His hands haven't been clean since they were covered with the blood of his mother's womb. Why should I go to his house, be seen with him, pollute myself? And now that I know how the thing came about, it's doubly humiliating. Of course, perhaps some post, some recognition might inspire me to work harder. Some people work by guilt alone.

Il faut réagir. This afternoon I rang up that blonde who gave me her number on the street. She was free, so I told her to come round right away. She wanted ten pounds in advance. I almost sent her away when I opened the door: she was covered with makeup and reeked of a cheap musky perfume. She brought along two white toy poodles. Nauseating, these women who think tiny dogs are chic. I didn't even offer her a drink; I simply waved the ten pounds under her nose and dropped them on the hall table. Then I took her upstairs.

I was nervous and afraid of dozing off. In which case she certainly would abscond with her ten pounds plus a few trinkets besides. Somehow they can always pick out the valuable knickknacks. Being in the same room with her annoyed me, the room where I sometimes sleep with Salomé, pretty and clean in her white pyjamas. Take off your clothes, I told her, and wash that filthy face too. You'll find some cotton and cold cream in the bathroom. I never do that, she said. You'll do it now. But without my makeup I'm not pretty. What ever gave you the idea you're pretty *with* makeup? I can't stomach lipstick. I suddenly felt violent towards her. I wanted to fuck her and have done with it. I took the cotton and smeared the lipstick all over her face to get that disgusting taste off her mouth, even if I didn't intend to kiss her. But when you make love, sometimes you kiss in spite of yourself. What's your first name? Her name was Irene. Eye-reen, really,

how monstrously vulgar. What's yours? I haven't got a
first name, I told her. Don't bother calling me anything.
It's better if you don't know my name, it makes things
much too intimate. But I know your last name. I couldn't
care less, I told her. Here it was, seven o'clock, and I had
to be with Mangiagalli at eight. I threw her on the bed
and undressed her without any help from her: she was
like a mammoth rubber manikin. Her breasts were big
and somewhat floppy, more fun to play with than Salomé's, which are minuscule. Very frustrating, it's almost
as if she has no breasts at all. I kissed her, of course, just
as I'd foreseen, my tongue down her throat. Then I pulled
her legs apart roughly. It occurred to me that the poor
thing couldn't have been less interested in making love
to me; yet partly because it was her job, partly because it
was the truth, she told me how handsome I was and how
much pleasure I was giving her. And I, like an idiot, asking her if I really did look like an underweight *heldentenor*. As if the poor whore knew what that meant. On-
ward and upward. Three minutes, because I came quickly.
Then, instead of sending her away, I set to fondling her
all over and several times must have hurt her because
she kept saying Easy, baby, easy, that's enough. Then, on
top of her again. I'm afraid of getting pregnant. My, my,
imagine a professional like you getting pregnant. If you
want more money, I'll give it to you. Afterward, I told
her to put her clothes on and kicked her out. But that
odor was all over the place. Irene. What a name. It's
probably a professional name. I took a bath to wash her
off and put on black tie. My cravat was all askew since
I'm completely incompetent about doing them up neatly.

Salomé always takes care of it for me. The idea of Irene disgusted me, her body, having had her on our bed, in our house. Salomé would never stoop to that sort of thing.

At dinner Atalanta talked about flowers with Ercolini, who was at her right. He too knew all about flowers. Waves of Latin wafted over the table: Platycarpa, Vesicaria, Penduculata, Arenaria, Emarginata, Florida, Glaberrima, Nitida. Eloise was seated at Tristano's left and on hers was Egon, clutching her hand, making it hellishly difficult to get food up to her mouth. Mangiagalli was at Atalanta's left.

"Evelyn's going to whelp tonight, I'm positive. She's already having pains."

"Tonight I'm going to do some divine things to you. I'm dying to. Aren't you?" (Egon-Q.)

"Will you shut up, for the love of God."

"Did you get my telegram?"

"No, what did it say?"

"That I was going to do some divine things to you tonight."

"Undoubtedly my husband read it then."

Ismene was quite awake now. She had on a short skirt with a print of emerald-colored flowers and was sitting next to Ercolini, Angela on the other side.

Ismene: "Absolutely not, I couldn't care less. Psamma: I

certainly don't know what it is. A flower, I presume. Anyhow I couldn't care less. And look at him, all out of sorts because I said something nasty about that *Manon Lescaut* the other night. As if he'd sung it himself. Dreary performance of a dreary opera. Just because he's good-looking is no reason to put up with his pouting." Ismene had on a green hat, a bit original as dinner costume. She announced her wig was a mess and she hadn't had time to take it to the hairdresser's.

"We haven't seen him for a hundred years."

"Who?"

"E., of course. I never met a man who was less visible."

"It's such a pity too, he's really the nicest man in the world."

"How about you, Eloise, do you see him often?"

"Only rarely."

"Mangiagalli, you know, would love to meet him. You must get them together one day."

Sandrino unexpectedly began talking to Eloise. He was in a poisonous mood. They'd met several times before, but Eloise hadn't yet figured out whether Sandrino pretended not to know her every time, or if he was merely absentminded.

"What sort of books do you write?"

"Novels."

"Really, do people actually read novels these days? I certainly never do, and it would never enter my mind to buy one of yours. I despise new books. Much rather stick to the nineteenth-century Russian or French novels. The only people who knew how to tell a good story."

"I love them too."

"Why don't you read them then?"

"But I do."

"No, I mean rather than write new ones."

Eloise had a great deal of admiration for people who could carry on like that. She herself would never have the courage, particularly without an audience.

"Would you excuse me please. Evelyn is about to drop her litter and she's determined to do it in my bedroom."

"Disgusting," Tristano said, resigned.

"Tell the maid to cover everything with old sheets and ring up the vet. Also get a few vats of boiling water ready. This Evelyn always whelps at the most inopportune moments. The last time was during my daughter's first communion. I was on my feet the entire night."

"I've a proposition to make," Ercolini said, lighting a cigarette. "A fascinating man called on me the other day. A Russian. Donny Golucky sent him round."

"Really? I know him," Eloise said.

"Then you can tell everybody what an extraordinary person he is. White Russian, you know. He says Petersburg instead of Leningrad."

"No, no, I mean Golucky."

"Golucky? What's he got to do with it?"

"You were just saying that he . . ."

"Don't interrupt."

"I'm sorry."

"Anyhow, this gentleman has been gathering documents for years tracing the exact location of a sunken Spanish galleon."

"The exact location of a galleon?" Eloise inquired.

"Yes dear, the spot where it lies under the sea. Now will

you quit interrupting me, otherwise I shan't finish. Now then, he says it was sunk off an island, one of the Canaries, Santa Cruz."

"Is it full of gold, this galleon?"

"Right up to the portholes. They took some out seventy years ago, then nobody did anything more."

"Why did they stop seventy years ago?"

"Everybody died."

"The ship must have a curse on it."

"Don't be such a clown."

"But I'm serious. These things with curses on them do exist. Take Tutankhamun's tomb."

"Well anyway. The Russian knows exactly where the wreck is."

The arrival of Edward interrupted Ercolini again. Edward was a tall blond youth who breathlessly insisted on seeing the hostess.

"She's busy with Evelyn. You'd do better not bothering her now."

"Who?"

"The bitch. She's about to have puppies."

"Tristano," said Ercolini, "would you be a love and put my friend Edward up for the night? I told him to meet me here."

"Of course, no trouble at all. Would you like a drink? Some sherry perhaps?"

"Sherry at this hour?"

"I'm so distracted. How about a whiskey then?"

"That would be an improvement."

"So?"

"So what?"

"So get on with the story about the galleon."

"Oh, the galleon. Well, the Russian's already been twice and taken pictures of it at the bottom."

"Was it photogenic?" Eloise put in.

"If you don't shut up, I refuse to go on."

"I *am* sorry," Eloise said.

"He needs a few hundred thousand pounds to get together a crew of trustworthy sailors and a boat. We've already collected about half. The idea is, each of us would contribute say ten thousand."

"I'm already convinced," Mangiagalli said. "I could bring in a couple of industrialists."

"When they bring up the gold, what's going to happen? I mean they won't let you bring it into the country, will they?"

"That's a bit complicated, but we have a barrister who's setting up a holding company in South America."

"What if somebody comes along and makes off with the gold right under our noses?"

"According to maritime law, the wreck is the property of the first person who finds it. Besides, our Russian will be protected by U.S. Navy reconnaissance planes."

"Who's authorizing them, President Nixon?"

"What if the sailors steal it?"

"Why should they? The thirty people who've put up the money are among the most influential in Europe. They'd never get away with it."

"I've chipped in twenty thousand," Sandrino said.

"Don't even consider it," Egon whispered to Eloise. "It's perfectly absurd. You'd think he was the first White Russian to perpetrate a hoax like this. And that Ercolini, what a nincompoop. Typical of him to fall for it."

"What if the wreck turns out to be a dinghy two people rowed out for a love tryst in 1933 or something?"

"The Russian is a bosom friend of Yousoupoff's."

"That's one hell of a guarantee."

"And of Ali Khan's, and Porfirio Rubirosa's, and Konrad Adenauer's."

"Well, his references are impeccable. They're all dead."

"If they keep up with galleon business, I'd like to know when I'm going to be able to get in bed with you."

"An extraordinary idea, it seems to me," Edward said to Sandrino. "One might make millions and millions. Ercolini's extraordinary. Such a wise man, so engagé. Just to think that a few years ago I was a playboy chasing one girl after another. Finally I found Benito Ercolini and sorted out my mind. Now we're living together."

"Absolutely, put my name down," Tristano said without conviction. "Only you'll have to explain to Atalanta, I can't. I've already forgotten the details."

"You know what, I'll send you photographs of the documents and then we'll arrange a meeting with the Russian."

"God, anything but that. Atalanta and I couldn't stand one more new face at this stage. We're much too old and anyway our acquaintance is too large. Quite apart from the relatives, of whom there happen to be armies."

"Do you think the project would interest E.?"

Eloise phoned E. from her room. "It's bedlam here. These queer people. Everybody's talking to himself. All right, so we all do it from time to time. But you talk to me. You know Mangiagalli, the Mafia man? I'd love to see the two of you together sometime. You wouldn't like him in

the slightest. He's really quite ugly. You'd be rude to him.
But he's so powerful. Then there's Bosanquette. You can't?
No, I can't abide him either. He's a vicious old bitch, but
fascinating. Atalanta, though, is divine. Yes, there are a
few other people. Ercolini. I agree, he's infantile, but he
thinks he's so important. Also somebody named Egon. No,
I don't think you know him. What's he like? Well, he's
hard to describe, he's just come into the room. I, with a
young man? You're out of your mind. Listen, I just called
to thank you. It was more than lovely, you know. Yes, it's
sunny here, but nothing at all like your place. Those
flowers of yours. I'd love to come back and see you. Monday? Really? How marvelous, that cheers me up. Do you
truly want to see me? You know, I'm quite touched. Also
hearing your voice. Do you enjoy me talking to you about
you? Yes? I'll be there on Monday. Goodbye. Then I won't
say hello to Atalanta for you, she won't know we've talked.
What? No, it's just that it would give her too much satis-
faction. I'll try very hard to be good. You too, though."

"That goes for you too, young man," Eloise said to Egon
who was kissing her on the knees.

"With you around, who can be good."

Eloise took his face between her hands. A kiss, first on
the lips, then the eyes. Beautiful Egon (Q.).

Now that I think about it, I don't like this name Egon
at all. Its sole good point is that it begins with a vowel. I
like the assonances it creates. Maybe I will call him Q.,
which is better.

"Where do you come from?" (Eloise)

"Take down your arms. I'm just here to borrow your
bath salts. Ismene is on her way to bed. I'll be back later."

"What's that you were saying about bath salts?"

Q.: "You don't seem to have any."

Eloise: "Quite right, I don't. But there must be tons of them in every bathroom in the house."

Of course if I definitely make him Q., it's the end of the E.-A.-A.-E. problems and the Eloise-Atalanta-Angela-Egon assonances.

Egon wound up again with

◇◆◇◆◇◆◇◆◇◆◇

That explains the telegram, if it's the one I read: Egon was telling her he wouldn't be able to come to let her know his wife would be there. Obviously they've established a code of some sort. "So that the human has nearly become an authentic fraud."* I went on reading Salomé and almost missed my appointment with Mangiagalli. I got there late as it was. He had on dinner clothes too: he was like an albino slug, doubtless the ugliest creature I've ever seen, a one-man revolution against pulchritude. Also thoroughly unpleasant to be around. In other words, not only was he mentally philistine and corrupt, he was physically philistine and corrupt. I introduced myself and, since I'm a pig, I was polite and gracious. He told me my wife was divine, which she is not, and that later we would pick up a friend of his (did I by any chance know Sandrino Bosanquette, the brilliant designer, the toast of New

---

* Musil, *Op. cit.*

York, the beloved of the theatre world?); then we would attend a party where we'd be given something to eat, we'd have a nice tête-à-tête, we'd get acquainted and talk things over. Everything planned out, in other words. Where was Salomé keeping herself these days? His guess was as good as mine, I said.

Sandrino maintained she hadn't seen my wife for a couple of months. The weekend is part of the fiction, then. But this time, what with Mangiagalli's phone call, I was convinced it was part of the diary. Or might it have happened just as she describes it two months ago?

Sandrino Bosanquette was tall and gaunt. Hair nearly frizzy, pointy eyes and lips, bitter voice, body and face. Instantly repulsive. Salomé evidently envies this old bitch's influence over certain people, the power to take or leave socially.

Let me quickly point out one thing: Sandrino Bosanquette and Erode Mangiagalli aren't these people's real names. I've used the ones Salomé made up because they're distinctive, and besides, you never know, damn it.

They are just the sort of scum I detest. If only I could start a People's War, they'd be the first two heads I'd decree superfluous. Miserable philistine swine, snobs, bungling morons. I didn't know Salomé was married, says Mangiagalli, a phrase he'd already used on Salomé, if not that weekend, then on some other occasion. Neither did I, I said. I didn't mean to offend you, he said. Neither did I, I said. I'm not offended at all, he said. Now what was that prick after? Is it because in life it's necessary to kiss ass to get ahead, and in the end he had kissed just enough people's to gain power over poor fools like me? What a

threesome: Mangiagalli, Bosanquette, me. A sweet idea
came to me: bugger that old hag Sandrino and make sure
Mangiagalli found out. The turned-down corners of his
mouth, frightfully thin, leered at me, lines of spite all over
his face. He puffed at a cigarette between two long gloved
fingers, and was dressed in frills and velvet. Go to bed
with Sandrino? How could anyone manage to get it up
over a body like that? I pigeonholed the idea. I felt like
vomiting. Do you write too? he asked. Too? Like Salomé.
No, I write differently from Salomé; I imagine you haven't
read my books. No, said he, I only read nineteenth-century novels. The new ones are unappetizing. (That settled
it, the weekend was no fiction.) Even your wife admits
they're unappetizing. Have you read any of her books?
No, but this is the sort of thing I know intuitively. You
can't know anything intuitively. Intelligent people, for instance, know only one thing by intuition, and that is that
nobody reads nineteenth-century novels these days. What
can people be telling you to make you so ill-informed? In
the 1850's Tolstoy could get away with explaining Anna
Karenina from only one point of view, as if one point of
view sufficed for one character. The same is true of Vron-
sky, the servants, the palaces, the opera, because in those
days nobody much had the chance to see those things. In
the 1960's, however, what with movies and television, people have seen damn near everything. You've got to give
them something new. And what would that be? Think
about it, sir, you who say you've got intuition. For one
thing, no chapters. Chapters were conceived because they
derived naturally from their content in the eighteenth century; in *Tristram Shandy* there are chapters only two or

three lines long. Later, in the nineteenth century, the chapter became more nearly the magazine installment, dependent on length rather than meaning. What then is the point of dividing a novel into chapters, since most books these days don't appear in magazines? It's become a mere convention, you see. Didn't that ever occur to you? —I'm not interested in the slightest. I gathered that; Mangiagalli even less. What are you talking about, I'm fascinated. It's my job, after all, to keep up with all new developments. A man like you would be a boon to any committee. Just an idea of mine. I wrote your wife about it some time ago. Which committee? I don't know yet, I'll give it some thought. Do let's discuss it at dinner.

The soirée was a fiasco. For one thing, there were far too many people. The hostess, peaches and cream, fat legs and fat lips, but still pretty, was completely undone by the hundred people she had invited. Not to mention by the people she hadn't invited, like me. I asked her to dance because I liked her, and then went back to talk to Mangiagalli, who by that time had set himself up on a platform to bask in the full light of his and Bosanquette's philistine glory.

There was a scruffy orchestra complete with Milanese tenor who squealed in a falsetto and didn't know the words to any of his songs, and got by mouthing them. The hostess kept telling them to play tangoes. She too was only interested in the nineteenth century.

> Set an shansong
> Kee noo ruhsamble
> Twa tuhnay

Mwa taymay
Noo veevoh too
Laydair ansahmble
Mwa taymay
Twa tuhnay.

I could have sung it better myself. Café tables scattered
around; a buffet of mousse and pâté. I must apologize, you
know, we were having so many people tonight we thought
we'd keep the food simple. But was she being facetious?
Or did she want me to think that ordinarily the food in
her house was even more ornate? Very pretty, her pink
legs, her breasts like salmon mousse. Eminently fuckable
lady. Especially her voice.

I hated those people, that place, the thought of owing
them anything. I didn't want to become Bosanquette's
vassal or one of Mangiagalli's many moral debtors. Or be
forced to accept a weekend invitation from the peaches-
and-cream lady who occupied herself slinking along on
those legs, with that voice. Or to go to Bosanquette's first
nights. The only thing I wanted was to go home. And in
fact, there I was, at 10:15.

"What I would like to do, you understand, is something
akin to the art of the fugue. . . ."*

"The musicalization of fiction. Not in the symbolist way,
by subordinating sense to sound. . . . But on a large
scale, in the construction. Meditate on Beethoven. The
changes of moods, the abrupt transitions. . . . All you
need is a sufficiency of characters and parallel, contrapun-

* André Gide, *The Counterfeiters.*

tal plots. While Jones is murdering a wife, Smith is wheeling the perambulator in the park. You alternate the themes. More interesting, the modulations and variations are also more difficult. A novelist modulates by reduplicating situations and characters."*

Eloise: "You woke me up."

Q: "It's late."

Eloise: "Let's sleep a while longer."

Q: "I've slept long enough."

"You're tickling me."

"Let's do some more of those filthy things right now."

"Don't be silly."

"Shut up."

"I want to talk."

"You're all soft."

"You're so beautiful."

"Get your leg out of my way."

"I'm going to buy you tomorrow."

"Tomorrow I'll adopt you."

"I'll lock you in a tower so you'll never get away."

"I'd never try to escape from you."

"But you'll have to wait for me night and day in the tower."

* Huxley, *Op. cit.*

"And we'll do these foul things night and day in the tower."

"I love that, what you're doing now."

"You like it so much?"

"Divine."

"Why?"

"Oh it happens to women, not to all of us, but sometimes this sort of foul thing is absolutely delicious."

"But why do you like it?" (Q.)

"Oh darling that's lovely."

Q.: "How much of this do you want?"

"Of what?"

Q.: "Of me inside you."

"If you would shut up, I'd be a lot happier."

"But you were the one who said you liked to talk."

"Not always not always. Oh my god."

Pause. Time to dismount and kiss a little. Q. had a highly distinctive flavor. Odd that he made love so well, with that baby face of his.

I just can't seem to come up with a properly defined hero. I've got to put in many more pages of E. And bring him into the dialogue more often. Everybody's always talking about E. Q.-Egon shouldn't develop into the hero. He's only an episode.

E. is by no means the ideal hero, because he doesn't belong. By definition. Neither to society nor to one or more people. For that reason, I've got to build up his character.

"I'm going back to my room now and I'll be back in the morning." (Q.)

"But it's already four o'clock."

"I'm afraid we'll wake up Ismene."

"You'll go to sleep and forget to come back."

"Then we'll do some more foul things tomorrow."

"I'm leaving tomorrow."

He hadn't come back by six. Q.'s lithe body. His way of not saying anything. His nasal voice. Making love with him. Overwhelming, the urge to do it again. She got up and brushed her hair, cleaned her teeth. Lord, she could still taste him. She crossed the sitting room into the darkness. There he was, all curled up asleep. His naked shoulders were just visible in the halflight, his head covered by the sheet. Lying there in a deep sleep. Waves of eagerness churned in her stomach; she thought of him inside her. She leaned towards the edge of Q.'s bed; he was asleep. Outside, the dawn grazing the curtains. Quick, hop under the blankets; embrace him tenderly. Oh Christ: a breast and long hair. It had to be Ismene. Obviously they'd switched rooms without warning her, how thoroughly out of the question. Ismene's naked back. It was so funny that Eloise started snickering. Ismene rolled over to face her, still in a dream. Half because she was curious, half because no explanation would do, Eloise amused Ismene till nine o'clock that morning, when Q. arrived to find them lying there, mouths together, exhausted.

It's quite possible that this actually happened, though in a way I can't imagine Salomé, who is so passive, in bed with another woman. Today I put the Milton translation into a manila envelope and sent it off exactly as it was to my publisher. So I'm being corrupted too. Nobody understands the difference between mediocrity and excellence anyway.

Salomé isn't coming home for several days, she tells me in a cable. This time she doesn't even palliate the news with an excuse. Last night, I dreamed I was in a room; in the middle there was a bathtub with Bosanquette inside, nude. Deafening din: a dozen children crying, nurses wringing the necks of two hundred chickens. MPs and Senators were circling the bathtub, champagne glasses in hand, saying, "Your health, charming Sandrino Bosanquette," and pouring the contents of the glasses over his squalid little body. Writers and poets recited their work and sprinkled his body with bits of poems they were writing extempore. The bath water and champagne soon reduced the paper to pulp. The sight of Bosanquette's body was shocking. His Excellency the Sicilian Minister, standing behind me, had on only a white dress shirt. The guests were murmuring; this sound mingled with the babies' crying and the chickens' squawking in their death throes. I had a dagger in my hand. I moved toward Bosanquette with a smile on my face, keeping the blade hidden under a towel. Bosanquette, who in the dream had metamorphosed into Marat, made as if to rise out of the slime to have himself dried off. I threw myself on his shriveled body and stabbed him many times. The blood flowed onto the paper mush in pink rivulets.

When Mangiagalli came after me, he was completely naked and held a club. I wanted to kill him too, but the phone woke me up. What a shame.

I see Salomé's marked small crosses at the corners of the notebook pages I want to read. I'll have to make sure they match afterwards, exactly as I found them.

ꙮꙮꙮꙮꙮꙮꙮꙮꙮꙮꙮ

Atalanta was absolutely unhinged that morning. Evelyn had given birth on her bed. Tristano had spent the night in another room, but his wife's and the dog's whining kept him awake. Mangiagalli, however, was all fresh. He had already read the papers, found two pictures of himself in a weekly, and was taking a stroll with Lady Sandrino, who was taking sketches of the Palladian folly for his new sets for "Lucia."

The aspect of the planets during the last three days of the week indicates more changes in your life. Saturn's influence will bring you a period of new experiences, offset somewhat by the influence of Mercury and the Sun.

Birthdays: Francesca Burton, Charles de Gaulle, Erode Mangiagalli. Clothes for the Action People. The Smart Set. Young ideas for beauty. New tricks, new trends London, Paris, New York. Fashion pure and simple. The people who count. Mangiagalli, a portrait of the man, the wit, and the politician behind it all. The most dashing way to look now. Under the influence of Paris.

Eloise found breakfast a bit of a strain. It wasn't until eleven, since the hostess hadn't slept a wink. Eloise didn't quite know how to behave toward Ismene. Nobody said anything.

"Eggs?"

"Pass the tea."

"Sugar?"

"I have been waiting the past three hours for my breakfast. What in hell is going on in this house? I suppose it's all on account of those mongrel bastards. Even the coffee is bitter. And look at this roll, it's clearly made out of cardboard."

"Would you be good enough to shut up, Xenia. Have some consideration for us."

"We might ring up E."

"What would we say to him?"

"We could tell him about the bitch."

"Which one?"

"The one that whelped last night, of course."

"That would go over well."

"You ring him, Eloise."

"I already have."

"You might have told someone."

"You were all with the puppies."

"Not all of us, not all."

Silence. Eloise upstairs. In her room she wrote a note to her husband.

"Dearest: Not for anyone in particular, but just in general. Otherwise, with you patiently and faithfully waiting at home, I lose all sense of responsibility for my actions and behave abominably. We won't see each other any more. But I've always loved you, even if I haven't been the best of wives. Yours, Eloise."

She rang up E. He was out as usual, but she'd see him

the following day. She left saying goodbye only to Ata-lanta. She wasn't quite sure where she would spend the night.

◈◈◈◈◈◈◈◈◈◈◈

It's the only honest thing Salomé could have done. The letter hasn't come yet but I know she's sent it.

I'd rather Salomé left like this, not after one of her scenes. Even if my book doesn't get finished. Anyhow she's not leaving me for some he-man who will screw her better or is more successful or powerful than I am. In the last analysis, without Salomé and her games, I'll be perfectly content. I won't know how her book ends. That's no great problem, I'll just buy it when it's published. I guess she'll go ahead with the "diary," only she'll have to give up the conjugal lie game. The sweet young thing abandoned in this populous desert called Life . . . God knows where she'll go.

I don't want to hear any more about the people she liked. This morning the paper ran a long article about Mangiagalli's death. It says there were no grounds for the rumors that he was crooked and had several suits in court against him; as for the gossip that he went round promising people money he never paid out, that was slander. Then it goes on whitewashing his career. There's a note about his birthplace and how he accrued his massive personal fortune. His brilliant rise in the Fascist party is, somehow, played down, but his post-war achievements in the Christian Democratic Party are stressed in detailed rhetoric. Then more about his prodigious career, so cruelly cut off. Well, well, Bosanquette must have managed to bump this one off, all right. Galloping enteritis, died at four in the morning.

I'm going to make a new life. I shall work hard, see friends, mine, real ones, but only when I choose to. Just a few, just to talk. In the long run, I'm totally self-sufficient, my income isn't much, but all I'm interested in is having a desk and a cot to sleep on. Perhaps I shall even be able to finish my book.

No more reading about Salomé as she imagines herself or writing about me as I imagine myself. I shall descend into realism, tell things from a single point of view, in homage to Sandrino.

What if I were to pack my cases immediately, put my notes into a trunk, and ring for a taxi?

Hello? A single, please. No bath, a sink would be nice. Breakfast too. Reserve the room for two weeks, then let us see. I'll be over in half an hour, I haven't much luggage. I'm lightheaded with this freedom, the hotel room, my book. Afterward I'll write anonymous threats to Bosanquette or appear to him as Mangiagalli's shade. I'll get my friends together and start a revolution.

Ring Ring.

Hello? You're where? Back? Look here, I'm on my way out, no I can't wait for you. But why? What do you want to see me for right now? Why are you ringing me up, you never phone me. All right, Salomé. Yes, we'll have dinner together. Do you want to go out or stay home? It's all the same to me, but I've got to let the girl know. It's all the same to me, really.

Click.

And so I'm the hero. This is how I'll become him. It always winds up this way when you write in the first person.

What about making Salomé's notebook into the hero? Because I might now be able to go on with it. I'd like to write a different book though: the novel as hero.

I might do That. Go on eliminating Salomé more and more and

Don Giovanni

∴

NOTES FOR A REVISED OPERA

For Mary

But of birth and position I've plenty;
I've grammar and spelling for two
And blood and behaviour for twenty!
W. S. GILBERT, *Iolanthe*

Guarda la lista
Di tutte quelle
Vaghe donzelle,
Ma troppo bone,
Che il mio padrone
Innamorò.
FILIPPO ACCIAJOLI, *L'empio punito*

Elles t'aimaient pourtant, ces filles insensées
Que sur ton coeur de fer tu pressais tour à tour;
Le vent qui t'emportait les avait traversées;
Elles t'aimaient, don Juan, ces pauvres délaissées
Qui couvraient de baisers l'ombre de ton amour,
Qui te donnaient leur vie, et qui n'avaient qu'un jour!
. . .
Et le jour que parut le convive de pierre,
Tu vins à sa rencontre, et lui tendis la main;
Tu tombas foudroyé sur ton dernier festin:
Symbole merveilleux de l'homme sur la terre
Cherchant de ta main gauche à soulever ton verre,
Abandonnant ta droite à celle du Destin!
ALFRED DE MUSSET, *Namouna*

The question of tempo in the opera [*Don
Giovanni*] is a burning one.
ALFRED EINSTEIN, *Mozart,*
His Character, His Work

On the Myth of Don Giovanni

❀

The list of versions of *Don Giovanni* is nearly as long as Leporello's catalogue of the Master's women. As we know him today, Don Giovanni was born Don Juan Tenorio in Spain in the year 1630, the brainchild of a monk, Brother Gabriel Tellez, otherwise known as Tirso de Molina.

Of course, tales describing a similar character existed previous to *El burlador de Sevilla y convidado de piedra*. But it was Tirso who gave Don Juan his enchanting bravado, his devilish spirit, and his mania for conquest.

Tirso's plot was altered considerably by Molière and the Italians. For one thing Don Juan Tenorio was not particularly cynical. Then the hero's invitation to dine is not acknowledged by the statue of Don Gonzalo; like any self-respecting funeral monument, it remains impassive in the face of such effrontery. After many misadventures, Don Juan is forced to take refuge in a monastery—which coincidentally harbors a statue of Don Gonzalo. Don Juan reads his ominous epitaph aloud: HERE LIES A STEADFAST KNIGHT AWAITING GOD'S VENGEANCE ON A TRAITOR. Then he remarks, "What nonsense. Would you have your vengeance thus?"—and gives the statue's beard a tug. Silence. "I shall expect you for dinner this evening. Then we'll be able to settle our differences, and we shall

see if your sword is made of stone too." Don Gonzalo's ghost
later reciprocates the dinner invitation with a banquet that
takes place in his tomb. The fare consists of vipers and
tarantulas; the wine, of vinegar, frost, and ice. Don Juan
gracefully accepts and shows no fear of descending into
Gonzalo's tomb to partake of the infernal meal; but his
politesse is poorly rewarded by Don Gonzalo. The ghost
not only drags him down to Hell, he doesn't even give Don
Juan a chance to repent. In Da Ponte, the Commendatore
is more mannerly; it is Giovanni who snubs him and re-
fuses to repent.

In 1840, another Spaniard, José de Espronceda, retold
the legend in verse, changing the hero's name however.
Don Felix, cruel and irreverent gambler, mistreats Doña
Elvira, and she commits suicide; later he murders Doña
Elvira's brother, Don Diego. Returning home from a night
of debauchery, Don Felix encounters a lady in a veil
weeping and praying before a cross. Entranced by the
lady's demeanor, Don Felix follows her through fantastic
and intricate terrain until he finds himself in Hell. There,
amid ghastly, macabre dances, in front of a coffin containing his own corpse, he is forced to marry the veiled
lady: the horrendous skeleton kissing him is, of course,
Doña Elvira.

Another Spanish poet, José Zorrilla y Moral, wrote a
Don Juan Tenorio in 1844. This doubly detestable Don
Juan runs about murdering people and behaving very
badly indeed. So badly, in fact, that his own palace becomes a mausoleum of the dead. The funerary-monument
maker, a sculptor whom Juan meets in Act II, informs him
that Don Diego Tenorio "had a son, an infernal abortion,

a cruel and bloodthirsty young man at war with Heaven and Earth. Nothing was sacred to this one, neither life, nor home, nor honor." Later Don Juan dines with Don Gonzalo. The dinner is worse fare than ever before: a plate of ashes, a chalice of fire, and an hourglass marking the time.

Ramón de Campoamor presents us with a Don Juan who's aged and impotent, a victim of wine and gout. Having decided to leave behind some spiritual testament, he posts letters to five of his ex-mistresses, declaring his fervent and undying love for each. A month later all five reply and—horror of horrors—they all turn up at once.

The Spanish critics insist that Don Juan is, and can only be, a Spanish character, and claim that Italy, France, and England have distorted his image.

Since the Spanish nature is gloomier than some, they are more apt to fix on death's attraction for Don Juan. The idea of dinner with a dead man is not new: to bring staples to the dead is a time-honored ritual in Spain. But the error and at once the originality of the French and Italian texts lie precisely in the *statue's* accepting the invitation. This is a sophistication which I believe changes the plot and contributes the quality of absurdity and cynicism that makes the theme so modern. Moreover, in the non-Spanish version, Don Juan is very often no longer the Donjuan-esque hero. His libertine obsessions notwithstanding, every time he tries to seduce a lady, he is thwarted, even in Da Ponte—apart from Donna Anna, though there Don Giovanni is forced to kill her father.

Among the first Italian versions is Andrea Cicognini's *Il Convitato di Pietra*. The date of writing is unknown, but it was first put on in 1650, the year Cicognini died. It is clearly based on translations of Tirso, though not many characters from *El burlador de Sevilla* have survived. Catalinón, Juan's manservant, metamorphoses into Passarino, a character lifted straight out of the *commedia dell' arte* and nearly identical with Harlequin.

Onofrio wrote still another *Stone Guest*, no longer extant but said to have been produced in Naples in 1652. It was turned into a music drama by Filippo Acciajoli, seen by the poet and painter Salvator Rosa in Rome in 1669. Queen Christina of Sweden was also present that night, and both of them were bored to distraction, as their letters testify. Carlo Goldoni wrote his *Don Giovanni* in 1736, Luigi Marescalchi in 1784. Bertati wrote the libretto for Gazzaniga's opera *The Stone Guest* in 1782; revised, it came to light again in 1787, the year that saw the first production of Da Ponte's and Mozart's *Don Giovanni,* which owes much to the Bertati libretto.

In 1660 de Villiers, an aristocratic actor and the husband of a leading lady of the period, imported Don Juan to France as *Le Festin de pierre, ou le fils criminel.* His *Don Juan* is so unlike its antecedents, apart from a shipwreck scene and an invitation scene, that it might be considered original. Villiers exaggerates Juan's tendencies, so that he becomes, if possible, even more depraved. The play has numerous secondary characters and takes place in Seville throughout.

Don Juan, who's eavesdropped on a love scene between Amarille and Don Philippe, finds himself enamored of the girl, a passion intensified by the tantalizing possibility of destroying the couple's happiness. Once he attains Amarille's bedchamber, her father discovers them together, and Don Juan, true to form, kills the poor man. In order to escape from Don Philippe, he exchanges clothes with his valet (as in Da Ponte); later he disguises himself as a pilgrim (to become the pauper's scene in Molière). Finally Don Juan has an encounter with Don Philippe and turns on him, killing him. In an attempt to get out of the country, he is shipwrecked and finds himself in Spain once again, where he comes across two peasant girls. After he has fled, his valet is left behind to console the two girls with the catalogue of his master's conquests, so prodigiously long that he can't bring himself to finish reading it. Meanwhile, Don Juan bumps into the statue of Amarille's father. The Invitation. Once in the tomb, where the banquet is spread out, our hero is unrepentant. In fact he commands his valet to describe to the ghost his seduction of Amarille. Along the precipitous path to Hell, Villiers has him curse Jove; for Jove, read God.

Villiers's text was doubtless Molière's source, though the latter used the Don Juan character to symbolize the spirit of a new liberal philosophy. In his *Don Juan, ou le festin de pierre* (1665), Don Juan is a seducer in name alone and is perhaps upstaged by his servant Sganarelle. Don Juan in Molière even stoops to asking what his servant thinks of him. Sganarelle: "In this instance, it behooves me to tell you that I disapprove of your conduct. I can't believe it is right to make love to everybody the way you do." Don Juan: "What! would you commend a man for attaching himself to the first female he falls in love with? . . . No, no, constancy is for fools alone!"

Molière's play opens on a conversation between Sganarelle and Doña Elvira's squire. "He's a brute who believes neither in God nor the Devil. The list of his victims would fill a tome, but sooner or later the wrath of Heaven will end his life of sin. As for me, I'm just his servant and am bound to be faithful to him." In Act II, Don Juan is rescued from the shipwreck. He innocently flirts with the two peasant girls. When Sganarelle announces the arrival of his foes, Don Juan orders him to exchange clothes and escapes (again, the episode Da Ponte used).

Two centuries later, in 1836, Alexandre Dumas *père* wrote *Don Juan de Marana*, a garish pastiche that the Spanish enjoy putting on from time to time.

Da Ponte's *Don Giovanni*, apart from Mozart's music, is generally looked upon condescendingly. Some scholars—though not Einstein—consider the text quite distinct from the music, while even the most cursory study of Mozart's letters and of the mediocre libretti Da Ponte made for other composers reveals that the texts of the three Mozart-Da Ponte masterpieces were conceived by Mozart himself. For that reason, the libretto of *Don Giovanni* should be studied as if it were the *oeuvre* of both Da Ponte and Mozart. (Interesting to note that Lorenzo Da Ponte was a monk—an abbot, in fact—and, as is sometimes said of Tirso de Molina, a libertine.)

Don Giovanni in Mozart-Da Ponte is, I believe, the highest distillation of all his forebears and prenotes the progeny. Don Giovanni is a powerful, sophisticated, cultured man, who has musicians in his house and pavilions in his park. He is witty and intelligent—a modern, fascinating creature. That he throws Leporello his leftovers to keep him happy is only natural: Don Giovanni wants a faithful servant who will follow and obey him, victim of his jokes and fellow rogue to help out when Giovanni plays them on other people.

Don Juan is completely foreign to English soil. Unlike Faust, he is a hero of the south. Curious that Tolstoy and Pushkin, straddling the two cultures, confuse Faust with Don Juan.

Sir Ashton Cockayan brought Don Juan to England for the first time in 1662. A hanged man replaced the statue. In 1676 Thomas Shadwell wrote a play called *The Libertine,* which had incidental music by Henry Purcell.

A pantomime version was given in Drury Lane in 1782, entitled *Don Juan, or the Libertine Undone,* music by Gluck (first produced in Vienna in 1761). Jane Austen saw it in 1813 and wrote to her sister Cassandra: ". . . revelled last night in 'Don Juan,' whom we left in hell at half-past eleven. We had scaramouch and a ghost, and were delighted."

Apart from this ballet and the Shadwell, Byron was unacquainted with the legend of Don Juan, and it didn't interest him. He was out to create a hero identical with himself who would condemn the hypocrisy of English morals. Byron's *Don Juan* had a trying early life. First published anonymously, it scandalized everyone. It had nothing to do with the legendary Don Juan, except that Byron *was* Don Juan. He had all the courage, aloofness, aestheticism, personality, and physical beauty to be him. Frederic Prokosch, in his biographical novel *The Missolonghi Manuscript,* describes Byron's first hearing of the opera at the Fenice: "that frightening work" inspired in him "numerous reflections" and "emotional revelations."

Byron's long poem, perhaps his *chef d'oeuvre*, makes not much mystery of Don Juan's being the poet himself and the damsels therein described, flesh-and-blood ladies. In a Rome letter of August 23, 1821, Byron wrote his publisher John Murray: "Almost all *Don Juan* is *real* life, either my own, or from people I knew. . . . Remember, I never meant to conceal this at all, and have only not stated it, because *Don Juan* had no preface nor name to it. If you think it worth while to make this statement, do so, in your own way. *I* laugh at such charges, convinced that no writer ever borrowed less, or made his materials more his own."

Don Juan follows Byron, on his voyages, we see him on ships, his locks blowing in the wind, into Byron's self-exile. And, of course, into bedrooms.

Man and Superman by George Bernard Shaw is at poles from Tirso's Juan Tenorio. Shaw's hero, John Tanner, is no libertine, rather he becomes the exponent of Shaw's philosophy. In his letter to Arthur Bingham Walkley, which serves as the preface to *Man and Superman*, Shaw asks Walkley, who had suggested Shaw write the play some fifteen years before: "The question is, will you not be disappointed with a Don Juan play in which not one of that hero's *mille être* adventures is brought upon the stage?" And, further on: "What attracts and impresses us in El Burlador de Sevilla is not the immediate urgency of repentance, but the heroism of daring to be the enemy of God. From Prometheus to my own Devil's Disciple, such enemies have always been popular." He goes on to talk of Don Juan as seen by Byron, of whom he disapproves, and by Mozart, "the master beloved by masters."

"Mozart's is the last of the true Don Juans; for by the time he was of age, his cousin Faust had, in the hands of Goethe, taken his place and carried both his warfare and his reconciliation with the gods far beyond mere love-making. . . ." Shaw also speaks of the "Doña Juana" of Ibsen's *Doll's House* as "breaking out . . . and asserting herself as an individual instead of a mere item in a moral pageant."

After *Man and Superman,* the air is still for twenty years. But in 1925 Don Juan reappears as the protagonist of a play of the same name by James Elroy Flecker. He began it in 1920, inspired by Baudelaire's beautiful sonnet. Since an enormous amount had already been said on his chosen subject, he began reading Gendarme de Bévotte's *La Légende de Don Juan* as well as Bévotte's collection of early Don Juan texts, then he went through all the other versions extant. The result was chaotic, since Flecker was reluctant to give up a single detail borrowed from this or that author.

The play is in three acts; time, the twentieth century. Caught in a storm at sea off the Welsh coast, Don Juan and a Welsh songster named Owen Jones (who tends to resemble Papageno more than Leporello) decide to abandon ship and swim for shore. Don Juan passes out, to be revived by an exquisite fisherman's daughter (Tirso's "invulnerable" Thisbe). Once back safe in London, he introduces her to his mundane social routine, the ancestral manse, the Savoy Hotel, in a word, to luxury (Byron's Don Juan). What's to become of a poor fisherman's daughter who hasn't the slightest idea how to behave in polite society? Obviously she must be abandoned. As in Shadwell, our hero is a snob: he will talk only to Lady

Ann (Donna Anna, only rather coarse to look at) or to
Lady Isabel (Ann's cute sister, a cross between Mozart-Da
Ponte's Elvira and Tirso's Isabel). He assassinates the
Prime Minister, father of the two charming ladies, because
he—a motheaten inversion of Neville Chamberlain—is de-
termined to start a war.

Coming to Act III, Trafalgar Square, Don Juan invites
the Prime Minister's effigy to dinner, as usual is accepted,
this time with a nod of his marble head. It happens that
Lady Ann has turned private eye and has uncovered many
of Don Juan's misdeeds, including his murder of her father.
Don Juan is therefore compelled to kill Lady Ann as well,
afterward effecting a liaison with Lady Isabel. The
father's statue comes to dinner and Don Juan ends in
flame and smoke. Again the story is an excuse for satire at
the expense of English society.

There's also Benn Levy's John Tenison (1937): this
time the statue is in Hyde Park and Elvira is called Eliza.

In Sylvia Townsend Warner's 1938 version, the ghost's
apparition is a *mise-en-scène* to enable Don Giovanni to
escape his many creditors and the irate ladies pursuing
him.

In my own *Don Giovanni* I've tried to modernize the
character, not on any basis in fact but to conform with
the essence of the myth. The eighteenth-century spirit
that transformed Tirso's Don Juan and informed Mozart-
Da Ponte's is, I believe, akin to the spirit of the twentieth
century. A cynical, disdainful enemy of convention is a
part of our times, just as he was of that era. I think
that, despite Shaw's bad opinion of Byron, the poet *was*
Don Juan, his sentimentalism and profoundly Calvinist

background notwithstanding. Precisely this puritanical upbringing gave him his exalted sense of "sin"; as Kierkegaard says, the Don Juan "can only be a product of Christianity," that is, of the sense of sin and the challenge of the forbidden. "A sentimental libertine is the worst of libertines," Byron would write. So he always had to force himself to play the role he had created for himself. In any case, I'm convinced that all Don Giovannis are sentimentalists. The aloofness is an acquired trait. It's curious too that real-life Don Giovannis are always attracted by their literary epitome. King Philip of Spain, who it is said was the inspiration for Don Juan Tenorio, used to go and see Tirso's play, in disguise. Byron was endlessly fascinated by Catherine the Great ("He pleased me so yesterday," the empress wrote about one of her favorites, "but today no more."), and describes her disapprovingly, yet entranced. Casanova ran to Prague for the première of Mozart's *Don Giovanni*. Sterne, in his *Sentimental Journey,* is avid for him. And Balthus, a modern-day Don Giovanni, whistles "Là ci darem la mano" the whole day long. Perhaps what Byron most reproached in Catherine the Great was that she bought her lovers, whereas the true Don Juan, a sportsman, seduced, and that was that.

The other, truer lady Don Juan, the Marquise de Merteuil of *Les Liaisons dangereuses,* has, as Macchia notes in his *Vita, avventure, e morte di Don Giovanni,* the instinct for aloofness and intrigue that challenges morality.

Don Miguel Mañara, a Don Juan who lived in Spain and died in a state of grace in 1679, dictated his own epitaph: "Here lie the bones and ashes of the worst man ever to walk upon this earth"—an extravagance among so many stones extolling the virtues of spouses and the goodness of the dead: the extravagance of defiance of convention.

Dozens upon dozens of versions: transfigurations in music, in verse, in prose, in plays, in farce: Don Giovanni will always fascinate people. The inscrutability of his character will make him immortal. He is perhaps the hero par excellence. The narcissistic, nearly effeminate ambiguities, the satanic complacency, the virility of his bravado bring Don Giovanni's character to life and make him, in his inhumanity, profoundly human.

G. S.

Don Giovanni

NOTES FOR A REVISED OPERA

DON GIOVANNI

Notes for an opera in two acts, scenes, and intermissions

DON GIOVANNI, *extremely promiscuous industrialist*
DONNA ANNA, *wife of*
DON OTTAVIO, *Neapolitan aristocrat*
COMMANDER E. ACCIAIUOLI, *Donna Anna's father*
DONNA ELVIRA, *lady abandoned by Giovanni in Burgos, Spain*
THE COLONNELLO, *retired Italian Army officer, now Giovanni's factotum*
MASETTO, *fiancé of*
ZERLINA, *soap-opera starlet*
TRAZOM, *industrialist*
PIETRO, *Giovanni's butler and manservant*
EMPLOYEES, SERVANTS, RIFF-RAFF

The action takes places in Naples, then Milan

Act One

❀

OVERTURE

He had got used to talking to himself. He was marching
back and forth in the garden of the Acciaiuolis' house,
stroking his mustache with the inimitable air of an Italian
Army officer. Except that the Colonnello wasn't Italian at
all. Though he lived in Milan to be near Don Giovanni,
the Colonnello was only Neapolitan.

It wouldn't be accurate to say he was Giovanni's manservant, since he wasn't paid. Whenever the Master called,
the Colonnello felt it was his duty to follow. At the last
moment, a cruise on the swiftest yacht afloat on the Mediterranean; a flight in his private plane; a weekend at one
of the houses Giovanni had scattered all over Europe—the
temptation to spend all his time with Giovanni was
irresistible, understandably.

Long ago, the Colonnello realized it was impossible to
keep engagements of his own and he stopped making them.
At any rate, the little rendezvous he might have had were
insignificant, since he himself wasn't important in the
slightest. Don Giovanni didn't ring him up for months at
a time—what became of the poor Colonnello was of no con-
cern to him. The Colonnello couldn't suppress the waves

of jealousy as he brooded over the people who took the Master away from him. . . . The time had come to find out what the man was up to.

SQUARRANCIONE, Enzo. Devoted husband of Gilda, beloved father of Emilio, Francesco, Paolo, Maria, Misericordia, Riccardo, Pauperrima, darling grandfather, dear brother of Arcadio, Mauro, Anna Carenina. Funeral service at Filippo Broccati Figli, 10:15 Wednesday.

STREPPANTINI, Erminione. The Ladies of the Naples Risorgimento Society record with deep regret the passing of their member Erminione Streppantini and extend their sympathy to her family.

SVALUTANTE, Giangiacomo. Beloved husband of the late Anna, devoted father of Maria Rossi, Catalina Valecchi, Pietro. Reposing till Thursday 9 AM at Gualdini Funeral Home, via San Severino 65.

TABANCHINI, Filippo. Association of 23rd Regiment Veterans, Neapolitan Cavalry, laments the passing of their beloved comrade, Lieutenant Colonel Tabanchini.

Reading the paper, pacing, waiting. How long a journey would be, he was never told. Always to distant places and the goal inevitably some woman.

Keep reading, you fool. ARE YOU READY TO BE A MEN'S CLUB MAN? CERTAIN INTIMATE DETAILS IMMEDIATELY CLASSIFY A MAN TO PEOPLE OF GOOD TASTE: NECKTIE, CIGARETTE LIGHTER, AFTERSHAVE LOTION. IF YOU ARE PART OF THE ÉLITE WHO TROUBLE OVER FINE POINTS, CERTAINLY YOU ARE MADE FOR MEN'S CLUB PRODUCTS. The Colonnello groaned. Deep inside, he knew it simply was not just.

The Master wouldn't settle for only one male companion —unless he happened to be cultivating a business connection. Giovanni monopolized the situation and allowed the other person to participate. MAN, MASCULINE FRESHNESS, THE JOY OF FEELING YOU'RE A MAN. A WOMAN SENSES THIS. But the Master often got bored, poor Master. Dinners at people's houses, black-tie get-togethers, swarms of guests: he despised all of it. Left to his own devices, however, he managed to keep himself entertained. Attractive, rich, he picked and chose, dumped what didn't amuse him. In the meanwhile, he made the parties concerned his own—never an obstacle, impressive as he was. Dominating women wasn't much of a challenge: he simply took them all to bed. Except the ugly ones, who irritated him. As for men, he bought the politicians and he owned the businessmen. He rejoiced in stupid people (the Colonnello was smart enough to act stupid); probably it was because they relaxed him. But he couldn't abide the conventional types. As for his own family, it was a passion to him. Because he was the head of it, of course. CHILDREN BORN TODAY TEND TO BE QUARRELSOME, AGGRESSIVE, IN FACT PIGHEADED, AND THE GOODNESS IN THEM CAN ONLY BE EXPOSED AND NURTURED BY A LIFE FREE FROM WORRY AND CARE.

HOW SIGNIFICANT IS THIS CURRENT CRISIS IN THE ITALIAN SOCIALIST PARTY? TAKES THE HARSHNESS OUT OF YOUR SHAVE, RESTORES ELASTICITY TO YOUR SKIN, MAKES IT FEEL FRESH, CLEANLY SHAVEN FOR THE REST OF THE DAY. A PARADE OF MASCULINE STYLES FOR EVERY OCCASION, FROM COUNTRY CLOTHES TO SUMMER TOGS, OVERCOATS, EVENING WEAR. STYLES CREATED FOR A PUBLIC THAT VENERATES FLAIR AS MUCH AS PERFECTION OF TAILORING. OUR COLLECTION IS BASED ON A LINE WHICH WILL SUIT NOT JUST THE VERY THIN BUT ALSO THOSE WHO HAVEN'T THE IDEAL FIGURE FOR FITTED

JACKETS AND TROUSERS. A NEW SENSE OF SELFCONFIDENCE. STYLE AND REFINEMENT DISTINGUISH OUR LINE OF MEN'S TOILETRIES. HAPPY DAY—FOR US MEN! FRESH, THE VERY ACME OF FRESHNESS. FOR A REAL UPLIFT, PUT A TIGER IN YOUR TANK. Don Giovanni's girlfriends numbered somewhere in the thousands: he'd had a different one nearly every night since the onset of adolescence. Models, actresses, countesses, duchesses. Aristocrats, peasants, idiots, boors, brains. The Colonnello had met quite a few of them. The Master devoted himself to them completely for an hour, an afternoon, a day, telling stories, charming them, mesmerizing them. He reveled in their company. Made love to them over and over. Then in the morning, the chase began anew.

Of course there had been exceptions. The Master had been rather fond of Donna Elvira for a brief spell. Her youngest child was his. He had a hundred children strewn across Europe. Elvira had tried to do away with herself a few times, after he'd abandoned her at a hotel in Burgos, Spain. The past few months she'd been chasing Don Giovanni like a bloodhound, turning up in the remotest places. Was the Master a narcissist? Well, not precisely. When you came right down to it, he was Narcissus. Or perhaps Aphrodite. Disguised as a skier, Elvira had tried to collar him on the snow-covered slopes of Courchevelle, Saint-Moritz, etc. Woman of the world in international circles, casino habituée, superlative horsewoman even by English club standards: to her, the Master was invisible, impossible to find. Unless he became the hunter. Barricades of secretaries defended his phones, trusted flunkies always said he was out, had just left. Impenetrable butlers, walls of silence wherever she went. She could tell by the silence where he was.

Neapolitan Workman Father of Seven
FALLS IN CEMENT MIXER
CHOPPED TO PIECES

COUSIN-LOVERS OF SAN REMO
Freed from Prison
Reporters Are Alarmed

JACQUELINE KENNEDY
Marries
ARISTOTLE ONASSIS

PHOTOGRAPHERS
Banned from Skorpios

Nepal Bridge Crumbles
90 Die

MARCANTONIELLI, Father Arminto. Our grief is deep and our loss irreparable. Father Arminto was the soft flame that illumined our congregation and our personal lives. He gave of his boundless love to his family, his friends, the Church, and humanity. Funeral services 9 AM Wed. Santa Maria dei Fiori.

It had turned too cold to hold the newspaper still. These infernal jokes of Don Giovanni's—and he was the only one who got a laugh out of them. A joke's not a joke unless at least two people are in on taking the victim for a ride.

As a matter of fact, in Naples the prerequisite for any practical joke is an audience. As is finding out whether the other fellow will put up with it. Also some sensitivity, enough to know when to stop . . . What attachments had Don Giovanni, what sort of ties? None, really. He was free: he functioned by intuition, not by reason. Don Giovanni was the most extraordinary man the Colonnello had ever met. A question of moths to the flame.

MAY 11 THIS YEAR, PEOPLE WILL BE CELE-BRATING MOTHER'S DAY IN THIS COUNTRY JUST AS IN OTHER COUNTRIES OF THE WORLD. THE SOLE DAY WHEN ALL MOTHERS' VIRTUES ARE REWARDED WITH KIND GESTURES, GENTLE WORDS, FLOWERS, GIFTS.

SCENE ONE

A garden in Naples. Commander Acciaiuoli's palazzo stage left, stone benches along the foot of the wall. It is past midnight

The COLONNELLO

Really. This was the last stinking straw. Here the man had dragged him all the way down to Naples for the night, only to vanish into old Acciaiuoli's house. Of course he was with the daughter Anna, that moron Don Ottavio's young bride. Appalling. Imagine, only a few days before, the Commander had arrived at the Master's office with vague ideas about selling his company. When all the Master had done was to ask him to lunch. The Colonnello hadn't been present, at least not officially speaking; he'd been behind a curtain (the Master's orders) eavesdropping. Giovanni'd done nothing but mouth commonplaces about trends in modern industry: "These days, it's well nigh impossible to stand up against European and American competition without enormous capital behind you. You've got to have nerve, my friend, courage, foresight to sell out before it's too late." Courage, yes courage. That was how he'd seduce the old bastard, make a heartrending speech about bonds of friendship between their fathers. Actually the Commander's father had never come far enough north nor Giovanni's father far enough south for them ever to meet, but the Commander wouldn't deny the relationship: just one more thing he hadn't known about his father. It would take all of four minutes to bring the Commander to heel. However if he turned out to be a little less primitive, Giovanni would scramble his brains with lectures on modern technology until it drove him to sign the contract. . . . In the end, a combination of things did the trick: the future of their industry, the future of Italy, the importance of tradition, of personal relationships in business. The Commander was dazzled.

Anna, the Commander's only child, was just leaving on her honeymoon but took the time to drop by and pick up her father. Insanely curious to see Don Giovanni, obviously. It was the only time they'd ever met, but was enough for Giovanni: the mere thought of possessing a virgin bride who was the daughter of a man he'd bought made his mouth water.

Now here was the Colonnello, standing out in the cold shivering. He pictured Donna Anna's luscious warm body; he's seen a lot of it in the glossies when she'd married Don Ottavio. The bedclothes all rumpled and Giovanni up to his ears in that sweet warm body . . . The Colonnello read on. PICK TWENTY FINALISTS FOR THE RUNNING OF THE CAMPANILE RACE. ANNUAL BUDGET APPROVED AT SORBOLO. NEW FISHERMEN'S UNION FORMED AT TRECASALI. The Master was shot with luck, had been since the day he was born. The overcoat the Colonnello was wearing was a gift from Don Giovanni and wasn't a bit well tailored. That's why Giovanni had given it to the Colonnello; everybody was always asking Giovanni for things and he'd got out of the habit of giving anything good.

SCENE TWO

The same

Enter DON GIOVANNI

His Master's Voice: "Where the hell are you?"
"Over here."
"Who were you talking to?"
"Myself."
"What have you been up to?"

"I've memorized the bloody papers waiting for you—in fact, I was just about to give up and leave." There wasn't a grain of truth to that. Even Giovanni knew it.

"Listen, friend, we've got to get out of here."

"Why, didn't you make it with Anna?"

(Giovanni's eyes had lit up at the sight of Anna's body; her heavy lips on his. Then came her father's unexpected intrusion. Scene: the Commander strides into his daughter's bedroom, finds Giovanni and Anna locked in a mad clinch, both stark naked. What had crept into the old man's mind, wanting to see his daughter at that hour?)

"The Commander's had a stroke, I can't wait around to be caught here in the Acciaiuolis' house. You never know what the papers will make of it."

"The old man's had a stroke? Is he dead?"

"Pretty close to it, I think, at least when I left."

"What brought on the stroke?"

"Well, one thing and another, business was bad, and then he was getting on, you know."

"Business? But you bought everything he owns and . . ."

"Enough, I don't want to talk about it any more. Let's go home, I need some breakfast."

The black Bentley engulfed Master and Colonnello and gray curtains fell to cover the windows and protect those well-known features from the world.

CONFUCIUS SAY, CHARMING COMPANY TURN LONELY SANDWICH INTO RICH BANQUET. "Have a piece of this."

"Are you out of your mind, me chew bubblegum? Don't you know it rots your teeth?" Giovanni lit up a Havana.

"Well, I only buy it for the sayings anyway," the Colonnello finished lamely.

SCENE THREE

The courtyard of Palazzo Acciaiuoli

DON OTTAVIO, DONNA ANNA, SERVANTS *carrying lights*

While the Bentley swung into via Caracciolo, Donna Anna put on a negligée and rushed into the courtyard, hair flying wild, face blurred with tears.

"He's dying."

"Who?" (*Ottavio, sprinting down the stairs stage right*)

"My father, idiot."

"What happened?"

"Shut up, will you please. Do something useful for once in your life. Run and get the doctor."

Scurrying in different directions looking for Donna Anna to announce that her father had just expired, the servants had, since Anna had fainted, to prop up her not inconsiderable body.

Don Ottavio (colorless man, tied down to his duties of Neapolitan nobleman, i.e. few) bent over his wife. Anna's beauty still intimidated him.*

---

* For years Don Ottavio had kept close watch over Anna Acciaiuoli—through her infancy, puberty, and adolescence. He'd watched her promenade with her governess. He'd always admired the way Anna changed her hairdo every day. One morning her long tresses would be gathered into a French twist; the next, they snuggled full and arrogant on her lace blouse. A third day, they'd cascade in swirls, a barrette bunching them at the nape of her neck. Only on their honeymoon was

Now, the sight of her wilted in the majordomo's arms aroused his desire—something he wasn't eager to admit in view of the somber circumstances. In spite of them, Don Ottavio noted, Anna had managed to pull on one of her most ornate wigs. Perhaps this fainting spell wasn't caused merely by the sight of her dying father; perhaps she was pregnant. His chest swelled with pride. Anna's hoarse, sarcastic voice shook Don Ottavio out of his reverie.

"What are you doing, standing there gaping at me? Didn't I tell you to make yourself useful?"

"What can I do, darling? Your father's dead and you . . ."

"Dead?" Anna fainted again, leaving Don Ottavio convinced he'd be a father soon.

The cook and a whiff of vinegar soon revived Anna. *Your holiness. Father, I cannot beg forgiveness from you and God. My sins are too grievous. How will I go on without my daily visit? Will I be able to survive without your absolution? In mortal sin, your child Anna. P. S. Will I ever return to a state of grace?—My dear child. The goodness of Our Lord is so great that He embraces all in His immensity. Return to Our Lord Jesus and humbly beg His forgiveness. God sees all and knows all. He hears your penitence and your desperation. Come to me and confess. Yours in Christ, Father Felix.* Laboriously Anna got up and dismissed the servants with a wave of her hand. Anna had an innate prepossession that Ottavio had always envied.

"How do you feel?"

"Not well. In fact, ghastly."

Ottavio able to discover that these transformations were attributable to an expensive series of hairpieces and wigs Anna attached by means of bobby pins to her very short real hair. But her large, sinuous body, her full, round breasts and buttocks had been no illusion.

She wanted some proof of his love and devotion: a strange thing to demand, all things considered. Of course he was devoted to her and would do anything for her. But why? Because her father's death had been caused by the treachery and sins of one man. Who?* She didn't know, but she was determined to be vindicated. Yes, of course, he would get right to it.

After exacting her husband's solemn promise, Donna Anna chose to faint again. Only this time the bobby pins didn't hold up and her wig met the pavement first. Before passing out altogether, Anna pressed the wig back in place with one limp hand, then closed her big, beautiful, black eyes.

SCENE FOUR

Don Giovanni's house in Naples. Clear dawn.

DON GIOVANNI, the COLONNELLO

Nearly a year had gone by since he'd been here last. Breathtaking view, tasteful rooms, efficient staff: he decided to come more often. In the heat on the terrace the

* Divination by oracles, *theomancy*. By the Bible, *bibliomancy*. By ghosts, *psychomancy*. By spirits seen in a magic lens, *cristallomantia*. By shadows or manes, *sciomancy*. By the stars at birth, *genethliacs*. By winds, *austromancy*. By the entrails of a human sacrifice, *anthropomancy*. By red-hot iron, *sideromancy*. By mice, *myomancy*. By a cock picking up grains, *alectryomancy*. By fountains, *pegomancy*.

Master's foul mood evaporated into the scent of orange blossoms.

"Get me a robe." The order was directed at no one in particular. The Colonnello came back with a white terry-cloth bathrobe draped over one arm. Everywhere beautiful things, embroidery, ashtrays, humidors, lighters engraved with dates, signatures, the names of Don Giovanni's houses. The same lotions in the bathrooms, the bars always stocked with decanters sporting silver coats-of-arms labeled vodka, Pernod, Martini & Rossi, Cinzano, Dubonnet, Fernet, J&B, Teachers, rye, Martell, Courvoisier, Chartreuse, aquavit. Luxury abounded. The Colonnello poured himself a clear glass of vodka.

"Fetch me one too." The Master's voice from the terrace. Was it possible he wasn't human? Eyes in the back of his head. When you were talking, you had the sensation he was listening to what you were thinking.

The Colonnello heard a loud splash followed by happy gurglings: Giovanni had dived into the Mediterranean. The sea at this hour must be icy. His arms curling along in a crawl, he shouted something.

Colonnello (*from the terrace*): "What's that you say?"

"On the next beach . . ."

"Come again?"

"A good-looking girl. Can you make her out?"

"What do you mean, make her out. She must be half a mile off."

"She's got a bikini on. She seems damn well put together. Send the butler over to ask her to lunch."

"You're insane. She won't come."

"Then you go ask her."

"Never mind that, I'll send the butler."

The man must have the eyes of a vulture to pick out a beautiful woman at this distance.

"Give the Master's name and perhaps she'll accept." The name itself was an aphrodisiac. Dripping with seawater, Don Giovanni rubbed himself dry on the bathrobe and downed his vodka.

"Bravo. You get more useful all the time. You're becoming a decent bartender."

"I feel rotten this morning, so lay off the insults, will you."

"I hand you a compliment and you go into a pout. What about the girl?"

"What girl?"

"The girl we invited to lunch."

"What about her?"

"Where in hell is she?"

"Be reasonable. The beach is a good way off. The butler has to get there, explain to her, she has to decide whether or not she wants to come, then she has to make herself presentable, and lastly she has to get over here. Give her twenty minutes at least."

"My God, where do people find the time to waste?"

SCENE FIVE

The same

Enter DONNA ELVIRA

Another vodka, which went down the wrong way when Donna Elvira made her entrance. Don Giovanni ran his hands through his hair in exasperation.

"My dear Elvira. So good to see you."

"I have been hunting for you for months. Months, do you hear. I write, my letters come back unopened. As for the phone, you've never been near one in your life, or so it would seem. The least you could do is make some show of pity. I don't mean to whine, but the best years of my life, truly the best years . . . I've been wandering around like a madwoman . . ."

"Well here you are, and I asked you to come."

"Only because you didn't recognize me."

"I hardly dared hope it was you."

"Liar."

The Colonnello moved for the door, anticipating a row, but a glance from Giovanni stopped him cold.

"Colonnello, please entertain Elvira while I dress."

Elvira drifted in the direction of the bar. She inspected herself in a mirror drawn hastily out of her bag as soon as Giovanni was gone.

"If you only knew how long it's been, Colonnello. Why did Giovanni leave me stranded in that town in Spain? Have you any idea? Not so much as a letter or a word of explanation . . ."

"Those things happen."

"A note . . ."

"The Master never writes notes or letters."

"He might have phoned . . ."

"He must have had his reasons."

"What?"

"Business."

"Business my foot. Women. People have told me some things . . ."

"My dear Donna Elvira. It's no secret that Don Giovanni has a way with the ladies."

"Spare me the details."

"But you asked me."

"Yes, tell me. Does he ever have affairs? I mean serious, long-lasting love affairs?"

The Colonnello Pacing Back and Forth Across the Terrace Shrugging His Shoulders from Time to Time and Waving His Arms Expressively

If I'd written down the names of all the ladies
Who have thrown themselves at Don Giovanni,
Truly, Donna Elvira, the roster'd take up
Twenty volumes. Once I thought I could make a lis
Just for fun, but their names began to slip my min

Escapades in France, in Italy, in England,
Not to mention the mistresses in Spain;
Models crawling miles to get to him in New York;
Prostitutes dreaming he'll come to them in Stockhol
Movie stars chasing him across continents.

He screws them all,
They fall in love,
He disappears.
What can you expect, he's simply made like that.
He's a man born free.
Women
Of every sort, every temperament,
Large and well-built, thin and petite,
Ladies of the nobility,
Sensible housewives, sweet young things.
Farm girls, thirteen-year-old nymphets,
Stenographers, willowy Dames
Of the British Empire, his best
Friends' sisters. Not to mention
Career women, brainless blond bombs,
Rich ones, poor ones, he makes love to them all.
(He even goes after old ladies,
Just to keep his hand in.)
Perhaps to have so many
Is to have none at all.

Ritardando, as I don't know . . .
the Colon- But if there's a lady in the vicinity
nello With- It's only a question of minutes.
draws And then . . . you know . . . what he does.

SCENE SIX

The same

DONNA ELVIRA *alone*

Her alligator bag, a handkerchief in hand. After she blew her nose, out came the mirror again. That Colonnello had a nerve, humiliating her like that; clearly he was jealous of Don Giovanni. And she'd suffered so, given up everything. Well, almost everything. The Colonnello must have felt a pang of conscience, otherwise he wouldn't have fled the room like that.

The truth was, he'd gone off looking for the Master, but he hadn't found him in the bedroom or the bath; Giovanni had abandoned him without a word. The butler told him so.

SAVED BY HER DOG
WHILE ATTEMPTING SUICIDE

Neapolitan Woman Shoots Self with Revolver

Dog Brings Police Before It's Too Late

SCENE SEVEN

Hotel adjacent to Don Giovanni's house

DON GIOVANNI, RIFF-RAFF

Once at the Excelsior, he headed for the bar. A waiter greeted him; some patrons turned to give him long stares. What's he doing in Naples, do you suppose? Whispers. They say he's in the process of buying the Burtons' yacht. Not at all, he sold it yesterday to Niarchos. A stage whisper: He's Pat Nixon's niece's aunt's lover. Shhh. Don't be ridiculous, what does he need her for, he's got hundreds of them. Shhhhh.

Don Giovanni: Good God, how tiresome.

Because he was well brought up and because he was tactful by nature, Don Giovanni never showed his annoyance. Impassivity punctuated with absent-minded smiles, smiles that never registered around his eyes however. The bartender watched him move off with a twinge of loss. The tip, the gratuity, his income was receding in the person of the Stupendous, the Magnificent, the Famous . . . Giovanni loathed the coarse motions of paying for things. The bill, sir; checking the addition; getting out the wallet—obscene gestures all of them. The inelegance and embarrassment of touching money was surpassed only by

the inelegance and embarrassment of not having it at all
. . . I'll send the car for the Colonnello and we'll go off
to Capri. It's sunny there and besides, I haven't set foot in
that house for more than two years.

SCENE EIGHT

Ballroom in the Excelsior

DON GIOVANNI, ZERLINA, MASETTO, working-class GUESTS

He glided through one of the rooms inside. The people
in the bar admired the way he walked, his clothes, the
elegance of his hands, his remarkably handsome physique.
Some more whispers and shhhhs and "Will you please
shut up, can't you see it's not Marlon Brando at all?"

A hideous ballroom with red hangings, filled with a mob
celebrating. Giovanni cast an eye around the room, scruti-
nizing a girl here and there, trying to find a single good
reason to stay in the room. The women were dressed in
fake Pucci blouses, fake Gucci bags, fake Schiaparelli
scarves, fake Ferragamo shoes—as if the real thing were
any more chic. Ah, but over there: a good-looking girl.
Big eyes, delicious full breasts under a white blouse. What
about the legs? Not bad either. She was less frumpy
looking than the others, eyes made up properly, an attractive air of aloofness.

*Dear Juliana. The strangest thing happened to me yester-
day and really I hate to write to people about this sort of
thing but I must tell someone. At my engagement party—
you know I got engaged to Masetto—it was simply out of
the question, let me tell you, all his relatives, all my relatives, each more vulgar than the one before—I was dying of
chagrin, not to mention boredom—anyhow, who should walk
in but none other than—can you guess?* Don Giovanni!
*God only knows what he was doing there but the strangest
thing was that he started to stare at me. Of course I was
already staring at him, you can't exactly keep yourself from
doing that, with him. Really, he is the most attractive creature. Remind me to show you some pictures I tore out of
Paris Match when I get back to Milan next week. And the
fantastic way he dresses. I never dreamed there could be a
man like him on this earth. Men are usually so homely,
either that or they're queer. And then the scads of cars and
chauffeurs and marvelous villas and châteaus he has—*

The girl avoided Don Giovanni's gaze and finally re-
treated behind her eyelashes. But she kept her eye on him
surreptitiously. Finally she worked up enough courage to
meet his stare dead on. The corners of her mouth went
down in an attempt to keep from smiling and she lowered
her head. Somebody kissed her on the cheek.

"Atttenzzzione." The grating Neapolitan accent re-
minded Giovanni where he was. He wanted to get out of
there and over to Capri as soon as possible. What in
hell had become of the Colonnello?

"Here's to Zzzerlina and Massettto, a thousand years
of (cough cough)."

More unfortunate southern Italian peasant toasts. Three

cheers, and things obviously were going to get worse. Don Giovanni was on his way out when he realized that the girl who'd been staring at him was the fiancée in question. That cast a whole new light on things.

He zeroed in. "How do you do," vaguely taking in everybody. Then he turned to her. "What's your name?"

"Zerlina." Good. Only one Z, she was civilized.

Champagne all round. He made small talk with Masetto, the fiancé. Then, "Why don't we all go over to my place on Capri?"

"But we'd be a bother, there are so many of us."

"Don't be absurd."

Parents, relatives, friends, children shook Don Giovanni's hand. It was a red-letter day for all of them.

Dear Signor Carli. I was supprised to receeve yrs of yesteday. I'm happy to here yr honer is about to get marred agen & you need a cook houskeper. & yr helth is good. Im hapy to say the same of myself, thank the Good Lord. Im hapy Miss Zerlina coud be in Naples for a few days. I herd she was. I wished she'd come by & see me. I'd of given a lot to see her. I mis her all the time. In my dreams she always calls me mama. I saw Miss Zerlina in the Troubled Tempest. She had a good bit one aft, nersing a nice boy who got the tyfoid in the flood. It was real hartbraking. Shell be a real big star one of these days, mark my words. Anyhow I bot a house hear. Its a bran new cottage with lots of son. All I have to do is fix up the top flor. Im real grateful to yr honer for the leter you rote me, all my best wishes & please give my love to dear Miss Zerlina wenever you see her. Always yrs sincerely, Erminia S.

Half an hour later the Colonnello showed up, all out of breath.

"It took you long enough."

"I came as soon as I could."

"We're taking them to Capri."

"We're taking *who* to Capri?"

"This rabble. I'm going with Zerlina. Get them moving."

"Just one minute here." Masetto, dressed in a poorly cut Nehru jacket that was passable because of his dark skin. "Zerlina's not cutting out without me."

The Colonnello handed him a glass of champagne and took his arm confidentially. The scene was suspiciously familiar. "Tell me, Mr. Masetto, is this an engagement party, by any remote chance?"

"You know it, man. It's *my* engagement party."

"Lucky you, so young."

"Listen, what I want to know is where that creep's taking her."

"She's in good hands with Don Giovanni."

"Listen man, hands are hands, and his don't look as good as mine, when it comes to Zerlina."

"Come on," Giovanni interrupted. "We're leaving. Get over to Capri whenever you can. Colonnello. Make sure we've got a decent meal waiting and bring out the champagne."

"You see? A reception in the Master's house . . . You'll see how beautiful it is, a terrace with a view of the Faraglioni . . ."

"Listen man, I don't care about those fucken rocks, I don't like Zerlina buggin' out like that with that creep."

"Don't worry, Masetto, I'll take good care of her."

SCENE NINE

Don Giovanni's house overlooking the Gulf of Naples

DON GIOVANNI, ZERLINA

"But sir, aren't we going to Capri?"

"We're stopping off at my house for a moment."

"You have a house here in Naples too?"

"Overlooking the Gulf. Splendid site."

The chauffeur helped Zerlina down. She felt a bit out of her element; she wasn't used to the luxury and the quantity of beautiful things.

"It's lovely."

"What is?"

"Your place."

"You like it?"

"Oh, yes."

"What do you drink?"

"Oh, I don't know . . ."

"Let's keep on with the champagne then."

Zerlina went out on the terrace. Jasmine and wistaria and orange blossoms trailing everywhere, as picturesque as if Don Giovanni had ordered them arranged.

—*I took my shoes off and was sitting with my back to Don Giovanni, gazing out to sea which is always an appro-*

*priate thing to do. He was chilling a bottle of champagne in
a silver icebucket. The thing was, he's so attractive and at
the same time so intimidating. I knew then if he wanted me
to go to bed with him, who was I to refuse. Would it make
Masetto jealous? He did seem a bit uptight, when you come
right down to it. I had the feeling I should have thought to
reassure him. But Don Giovanni didn't even touch me, in
the car. A hand, an arm—there are a thousand ways to get
the point across, after all. But he hadn't done a thing. I
began to think I'd been overoptimistic—*

He'd spoken. He'd asked her some question. Did he
really leave something behind? It was just an excuse,
wasn't it? Actually he hadn't even said he'd left something
behind. He was after her, wasn't he?

He touched her shoulder and handed her a glass of
champagne.

"Have you known each other long?"

"Who?"

"Masetto."

"Oh, since we were born. Until now we were too young
to get married."

"What's it like, living here in Naples?"

"I don't. I live in Milan."

"And you came all the way down here to get married?"

"I'm trying to talk Masetto into moving up north."

"What do you do in Milan?"

"I'm an actress. In the afternoon TV serials."

"How do you like it?"

"Only so-so. The routine is boring, the scripts are atrocious. But it's better than doing nothing at all. Anyhow, I
need the money."

"What does your father do?"

"He's dead."

"What a bore, the fathers are always dead. Where did he die?"

"In Russia."

"I was in Russia too."

"You were in the war?"

"Actually no, I barely escaped that, a bit of arranging, a bit of good luck. And I occasionally wandered off to Vienna or Bucharest. Stupendous city, that. Do you know Bucharest?"

"No."

"It was like going back to the Belle Epoque. Like escaping from Hell. They gave sublime balls, tribes of magnificent women. And Budapest, that was another dream. As if there were no such thing as a war going on. Luxury out of control."

His concentration on her was so intense that Zerlina began to feel nothing else in the room could attract his attention away from her. Terrace and champagne swirling around in her head. The tickle of bubbles licking her tongue. A wistaria branch floated across her forehead. Poor Masetto, all alone. What a weird situation, her and Don Giovanni. She crushed an orange blossom and sniffed at it.

Was she boring him? Down we go, more bubbly, what else was there for it? One solution. Now don't get drunk, it won't help. His voice. There, he's gazing out to sea too, he's thinking. What about? Not you, that's for sure. You, Zerlina, soap-opera star, the housewives' Greta Garbo, the cleaning ladies' Marilyn Monroe. He told you not to say anything. Well, if he'd caught my eye, I would have told *him* a thing or two, for instance he had no right saying that, telling me to shut up. If you have any sense at all, you'll get on the phone to Masetto and tell him you'll leave him for him. Whom for whom? You're crocked, no doubt about it, and will you please stop making up internal dialogues and talk to this man, who is much more interesting.

"Do you ever go back to Bucharest or Budapest or wherever it was you said you went?"

"No, now Hong Kong's the place. In a sense those cities reshuffled the century. What I mean is that they were an oasis of insanity during the war. Not that the war was sane. Hong Kong, it's insane too, marvelous. You ought to go there sometime. Have you ever been?"

"Me, to Hong Kong? No, never."

"Do go sometime. Though Budapest doesn't exist any more. Neither does Warsaw."

"What? But that's not true, they make marvelous movies there and the theatre's very good, I'm told."

"Nonsense, they haven't the sense to put anything together well. Gruesome, lugubrious pastiches."

She was very sure of herself, he thought. She held her glass rather vulgarly. Damn pretty though.

"Come, let me show you around." He took her arm and led her to the edge of the terrace. The sea below was still, green, luminous, full of stars and jewels.

Here we go, he's taken your arm. How are you going to get up the nerve?

He squeezed one of her hands and brought it toward him. The most beautiful part of making love is the beginning. The back trembles, the stomach shrinks, the faces come together. My, that handsome face. Those enormous eyes. His mouth is warm, just the slightest bit moist. His sinks onto yours. His arms wrap around your back, your legs weaken: the excitement of his nearness. These things should always be like this. Mouths, teeth. Hours and hours of it.

Your hands travel across his face, that magnificent face; touch his neck. Your blood is rushing to your breast. Come, he says. —*Of course I was going with him, wild horses couldn't have stopped me. To go to bed with a man like that is a once in a lifetime proposition, I'm sure you agree. You can't imagine how exhilarating, to have him inside you. Sorry, I don't mean to be pornographic, but you know what I mean. Anyhow, I was debating whether to let him know straight off what I felt for him or to put up a fake fuss. I decided that modesty wouldn't appeal to him at all; but there was still this niggling in the back of my mind that I really shouldn't, what with Masetto and the whole way you're brought up, you know. Of course the thing about Masetto is that he probably would have been mad at me if I hadn't. In the end curiosity got the best of me. We were both fascinated with each other's bodies and—*

His bedroom, behind louvers and curtains of wistaria and jasmine. He wouldn't let her undress, except to let her full, bronzed breasts out of her blouse. Fast and furious, in a hurry to take her, without talking, either of them, on top of the sheets, probing with his fingers, his hands on her stomach. Let me see you. Just a minute. Then he threw himself on top of her.

SCENE TEN

The same

Enter DONNA ELVIRA

Behind a wistaria branch, silhouetted against the sun, the shape of a woman. Zerlina was the first to glimpse it.

"Did you leave something behind?" Giovanni asked wearily.

Who was she? Did he know her? He'd suddenly gone cold. Was she his wife? A mistress?

—*Well, needless to say I was paralyzed with embarrassment. I picked up my clothes and decided to get out of there fast. The woman stepped in front of the door to cut me off. Don Giovanni stayed right where he was, stark naked on the bed. The situation really turned him off, you could tell.*

"My dear child, you are so young," the woman said taking Zerlina's hand. "It shows, just a mere child. Perhaps you don't know who this man is. Or how he'll make you suffer. I gave the best years of my life to him, only to be humiliated. Dear child, now, while you are still innocent, you must get away from this monster, before it's too late."

What was this dreary woman doing, butting her nose in here? Of course she wasn't continuing with Don Giovanni any longer than this afternoon, in fact she never expected to see him again. Even so it was worth every second. Quite apart from that, what right had this woman to say things like that in front of a man whose respect she could only lose?

"She's out of her mind," Don Giovanni pronounced from the bed, smiling. He hadn't budged.

Donna Elvira was sobbing in an armchair. How disgusting. *Not my style, I told myself. I had to get out of there. It upset me to ditch Don Giovanni like that, but I had to catch up with Masetto on Capri as soon as possible. It would have been stupid of me to lose him too.*

INTERMISSION

INGREDIENTS THAT PRESERVE YOUTH BY PROMOTING THE CLEAN AND EFFICIENT FUNCTIONING OF YOUR VITAL ORGANS. NIGHTTIME'S THE RIGHT TIME FOR LOVEMAKING AND USING OUR CREAM. A SOFT SOFT EMULSION, A NATURAL PERFUME, ACTIVATED AND DISPERSED BY THE TEMPERATURE OF YOUR BODY, SURROUNDING YOU WITH A CLOUD OF PERSONALITY. PRECIOUS CALAIS LACE CUPS SHOW OFF THE TRUE CURVATURE OF YOUR BREASTS. SHE HOSTED FRIENDS AND RELATIVES FROM ALL ACROSS EUROPE IN AN INTIMATE ATMOSPHERE OF AN EXQUISITELY TASTEFUL BUFFET. DOUBLE DEODORANT ACTION ELIMINATING DISAGREEABLE ODOR AND ITS CAUSE IN ONE DAILY APPLICATION.

SCENE ELEVEN

The same as Scene Ten

DON GIOVANNI, *later* DONNA ANNA, DON OTTAVIO

It infuriated him. That ass Elvira picking the precise instant to come barging in. And then Zerlina scampering off like a scared rabbit. But probably he could catch up with her on Capri, if she wasn't a complete birdbrain. Easy enough to escape Elvira, who hadn't moved from the armchair and was still howling. He skipped down the stairs in the sea wall. Suddenly he spotted Donna Anna and Don Ottavio trudging up towards him. The sight inspired a wave of depression.

Ottavio: We'd like a word with you.

Giovanni: Would you mind if we talked later? Actually I'm in rather of a rush right now.

SCENE TWELVE

The same

Enter DONNA ELVIRA

Eyes puffy and red, here the old bore was again. At the most inopportune moment possible, as usual.

Elvira: My dear woman, take care (*sob*) you don't know (*sob*) this man (*sob*) you've no idea (*sob*) he's out to ruin womankind.

How dare this woman Anna had never met before make allegations about what had gone on between her and Giovanni. She cast him a glance out of the corner of her eye and saw him smiling over clenched teeth, obviously losing patience. He was the most desirable man: those kisses, that shudder . . . She began to hate Ottavio and this pest of a woman making all that noise. But what was she going to tell Father Felix? He'd get it all out of her eventually. Don Giovanni . . . had been the cause of her father's death. His mere presence emphasized how ridiculous Ottavio was: fat, squat, his tiny mustache creeping toward his fleshy red lips.

"Who is this woman? Giovanni, do introduce us," said Don Ottavio.

"Just the neighborhood psychotic. I'd ignore her, if I

were you. Let's have a quick glass of champagne now
and get together later."

"He seduced me," Elvira shrilled. "He took me away
with him, I abandoned everything for him, my house, my
husband, my children. Now he won't even look at me. He
deserted me. Imagine it, in Burgos, Spain. Not even in a
city where there's something to do or look at."

"She doesn't seem particularly crazy," Ottavio said
charitably.

"Ah but she is. Been loony for years. From time to time
she even does away with people."

"It's he who's psychotic, he's a pathological liar, he's a
sex maniac." Subtle woman, that Elvira, reduced to sobs
again. She raised her soggy handkerchief to hide her face
and stumbled up the stairs toward the house.

"Excuse me please. I wouldn't want her to do anything
foolish. It wouldn't be the first time." If Elvira was up
there sniveling and taking her customary ineffectual dose
of barbiturates, Don Giovanni wasn't having any part of
it. Nor was he eager to stay there with Anna and Ottavio.
He was on his way to Capri.

SCENE THIRTEEN

The same

DONNA ANNA, DON OTTAVIO

Her sombre eyes: he took her hand. Anna shook him
off. "What's wrong?" he asked.

She could see the yacht clearly: it had just pulled away from the dock, Giovanni on board. He was leaving her behind. Steaming off into the distance. "That night . . . my father . . ."

"It's getting late," Ottavio noted nervously. Something was coming and he didn't like the sound of it.

"How can I ever tell you, Ottavio?" She stared at her hands. "The door of the room squeaked open. A man came in and I thought it was you." (Giovanni would love that, being mistaken for Ottavio.) "He came towards my bed and started to—well, you know, make overtures. Suddenly I realized it wasn't you at all. I screamed, I managed to get free, I tried to get help and my father came. He recognized Don Giovanni . . ."

"Don Giovanni?" Ottavio clutched Anna's hands to his heart, paralyzed with grief.

"Then Don Giovanni escaped. I ran out to find you, leaving Father dying on the rug. I want you to know this and I want you to avenge our family honor."

"My dearest, my love . . ."

"None of that dearest-love business. Swear to me."

"I do, I swear it. But what is it you want me to do? After all, he *is* Don Giovanni, and then your father was no spring chicken. . . . That lady, what's her name, Donna Elvira, was really pathetic, don't you think . . . It must be very easy to fall in love with a man like him, don't you think . . ."

SCENE FOURTEEN

The same

Donna Anna *alone*

He hadn't so much as looked at her, he was so eager to get off the spot. And she'd made such an effort to dress just right; her makeup alone had taken half an hour.

Dear Soul in Pain. Your letter wasn't very clear. I couldn't make out what exactly it was that happened to you, and then that reference to "corrupting influences" . . . It could very well be that all the blame does lie with the man, but my dear child, have you examined your conscience carefully, bearing in mind that purity, chastity, and continence are the strong woman's virtues? If you are one of my faithful readers, as you say you are, you will recall how many times your Countess Beatrice has emphasized this truth. Give yourself wholly to your husband. Forget this other man. And above all, consult your Father Confessor.

CONSULT MEDIUM PEDRAZZINI. YOUR PAST REVEALED TO CONVINCE YOU OF ACCURACY OF PREDICTIONS.* YOUR FUTURE

---

* Divination by a wand, *rhabdomancy*. By dough of cakes, *crithomancy*. By salt, *halomancy*. By a balanced hatchet, *axinomancy*. By a balanced sieve, *coscinomancy*. By dots made at random on paper, *geomancy*. By pebbles drawn from a heap, *psephomancy*. By writings in ashes, *tephramancy*. By nails reflecting the sun's rays, *onychomancy*. By the mode of laughing, *geloscopy*. By ventriloquism, *gastromancy*. By walking in a circle, *gyromancy*. By dropping melted wax into water, *ceromancy*. By currents, *bletonism*.

SECURE THROUGH KNOWING. SATURDAY THROUGH TUESDAY. DAY AND NIGHT. CORSO GRANCAGNOLINO 756. TEL 431-850.

And she'd even put on perfume. For him, for Don Giovanni.

SCENE FIFTEEN

Aboard a yacht speeding toward Capri

DON GIOVANNI, *later* the COLONNELLO *at the dock*

CLAUSTROPHOBIA PREVENTIVES

His was probably the most famous on the Mediterranean. It wasn't as beautiful as the *Creole* or as huge as the *Christina*, but it was the fastest of the lot: 50 knots an hour. On the second deck, a small helicopter. Hanging from winches, two motor launches. If one pressed a button on the captain's bridge, a mechanism was set in motion: the stern of the boat yawned open and vomited out, amid smoke and splashes, a black fiberglass speedboat, flat, maneuverable, 80 knots an hour. As for land, there were two cars stored in the hold.

Don Giovanni at the stern gazed into the whiteness of the foam, the churning of the wake.

The Colonnello was waiting for him at the dock. "You'll never guess what just happened."

"Zerlina turned up, I should imagine."

"Correct."

"She was agitated."

"Correct. And?"

"Elvira turned up too."

"Blast you. You always know everything. All right: what did Elvira say?"

"The usual bit about my deserting her and refusing to recognize her bastard."

"Go to the head of the class."

"Now I have one for you: what did you do with Elvira?"

"I took her aside and informed her you'd be waiting for her at Marina Piccola. And that you were taking the late air ferry from Naples. That way we'll be free of her for the evening."

"Brilliant. Now let's have a good time. Some pretty girls. Are they all drunk yet, I hope? I've had one too many dull episodes today. I deserve a bit of enjoyment and relaxation." He finished the champagne handed to him by a steward and tossed the glass into the water.

Bored as usual, the Colonnello noted. The chauffeur was waiting to take them up to the villa.

SCENE SIXTEEN

Don Giovanni's terrace garden on Capri. In the background, a palatial villa lit up; pavilions on either side. Sounds of music and laughter

ZERLINA, MASETTO

"I swear to you."

"Hands off, you're contaminating me, bitch."

"What do I have to do to prove nothing at all happened between us?"

"You make me vomit. Whore."

"Oh come off it, Masetto. You're being an ass."

"Shacking up with him in front of everybody . . ."

"He didn't set so much as a finger on me. Now if we can't trust each other after all these years . . . You never had such a vivid imagination when you were a kid. Come on, Masetto, kiss Lina and let's make up, huh?"

Zerlina's husky voice warming, exciting him. She was a good-lookin' mother, that one. He started to take her in his arms and jumped at the sound of a voice. Don Giovanni.

"What's that?"

"Hah, now when he comes over here, we're going to see just what went on between you two. Look at you, you're about to blow your mind."

"Not at all. It just embarrasses me, his catching us together."

"Since when are you such a prude? Okay, I'll hide-and-see."

"Will you stop acting like a child."

"Doesn't look so good for you, Lina baby . . ." He faded into the darkness.

Don Giovanni: his luminous, smiling face. "And what are you hiding here for, Zerlina, all by yourself?"

She didn't want to lose Masetto, but on the other hand she wanted Giovanni too. "Leave me alone."

"Are you angry with me? Because of that witch? Come with me. Come over here." He took her by the arm and she squeezed his hand. Suddenly he spotted Masetto. "Now what are you doing, lurking over there? Come on, you two, stop necking out here and join the others. After all, the dinner's in your honor." Just as anxious as Zerlina to keep Masetto from finding out.

SCENE SEVENTEEN

The terrace garden

ZERLINA, MASETTO, DONNA ELVIRA, COUPLES *dancing*

Zerlina had only seen furniture that ornate in museums. A record player blared out on the balcony. Intricate terracing graded down to the water's edge. An exhilarating flying sensation, being up this high. The sunset lit up the immense window and gilded the chairs' wood. *Only you can make the sun go round, only you-hoo-hoo* . . . Among the dancing couples, Donna Elvira making a nuisance of herself, as usual. *Et maintenant, que vais-je faire, vers quel néant* . . . Zerlina asked Masetto to dance with her. *You're the tops, you're Napoleon Brandy* . . . Elvira had spotted Zerlina too. That meant Giovanni couldn't be far behind. *You're the tops, you're the Colosseum, you're the tops, you're the Louvre Museum* . . . Making her cool her heels at Marina Piccola for an hour;

could it be her presence irritated Don Giovanni? *I want to hold your hand* . . . Perhaps, though, he respected her unconventionality, her making it clear the way she felt. *And when I touch you I feel happy, inside* . . . But then again, it might be that she was making a fool of herself.

SCENE EIGHTEEN

The same

Enter DON GIOVANNI, the COLONNELLO

Elvira saw Don Giovanni dart toward Zerlina.

"May I dance with the guest of honor for a while?" Masetto relinquished Zerlina without a struggle. How could he not be jealous, Elvira wondered. A man like Giovanni was a threat to all other males. *Picture yourself in a boat on a river* . . . The Colonnello moved in. "Masetto, come with me. I'd like to talk to you."

"I've got nothing to say to you, fly, so buzz off."

Lucy in the sky with di-yamonds . . .

"I'd like to show you something, actually."

"Listen man, I've seen a lot of things."

"It's a marvelous picture."

"Man, you got one right over there, that bastard balling my chick."

"No, I mean a painting."

"I don't go for painting."

"What *do* you like?"

It was fascination I know, seeing you alone in the moonlight last night . . .

"What I'd like to do is take Zerlina home and shack up with her myself.—Somebody take that fossilized platter off the machine!"

"That seems sane enough, on the day of your engagement. But since you're a guest here, come along and I'll show you the house."

Lovely Rita, Meter Maid, nothing can come between us . . .

SCENE NINETEEN

The same

DONNA ELVIRA, DON GIOVANNI, ZERLINA, DON OTTAVIO, DONNA ANNA

But that troublemaking Elvira had surprised them again. They'd been all intertwined, happy, warm, cuddly. They were headed for the beach. And heaven knows how Don Ottavio and his wife managed to sneak up on them too. Both ladies began shrieking at the same instant. Giovanni had beat it in his motorboat. And Zerlina, she was making this a habit, had disappeared again, before Don Giovanni had been able to take, love, possess, and later manipulate her.

Act Two

❀

OVERTURE

After his problems the day before in Naples, Don Giovanni had decided to sell his real estate there lock, stock and barrel—the house with the view of the Gulf of Naples and the villa on Capri both. News of the Commander's death was all over the papers.

The papers Don Giovanni owned were exceptionally assiduous in their coverage of Commander Acciaiuoli's death. They described his virtues, civic acts, community spirit, sobriety and dedication to his work with unimpeachable diligence. They did not however announce that Commander Acciaiuoli had sold his entire holdings to Don Giovanni a few days previous.

Milan, STAFF EXCLUSIVE.—This morning a memorial service was held at the new Cesarino Trazom Industrial Center in honor of Commander E. Acciaiuoli, who died suddenly yesterday in Naples. His widow and daughter flew up from that city to place a wreath at the foot of the statue of the Commander in the Trazom Industrial Center Garden.

The statue, commissioned by Trazom some years ago

in gratitude for beneficences rendered him by Commander Acciaiuoli, is a modern piece executed in Carrara marble by the Realist sculptor Carmelo Pupuzzi, also of Naples. The widow, Donna Tilde Acciaiuoli, wore a black crepe dress and a black velour hat. The daughter, who placed the wreath, wore dark gray.

Trazom and the Mayor of Milan spoke of the grievous loss to Italian industry and described at length the achievements of the deceased. The Mayor took occasion to congratulate Trazom on the new Industrial Center, which will be inaugurated this evening.

Under Papal Benediction
Commander Ermanno Acciaiuoli
died tragically yesterday. He is survived
by his wife Donna Tilde and daughter
Donna Anna Teobanzi Acciaiuoli Crescente.

In the Peace of Our Lord
Rests the Honorable Commander
ERMANNO ACCIAIUOLI
His Employes, Workmen, Friends, and
Dependents Mourn His Passing. The
Administrative Council, the Syndicate
Trustees, the Management of CPIK,
SSTV, SIMO, SAZ, CAM, and CIV.

The Entire Personnel of CAIT
Mourn the Passing of
Commander Acciaiuoli and
Offer Condolence to
His Family

SCENE ONE

Don Giovanni's duplex penthouse in Milan

DON GIOVANNI, PIETRO

A perfumed bath was waiting for him. Pietro brought in his mail.

"Any phone calls?"

"I left all messages beside the telephone."

"Read them to me."

"I can't. Some of them are personal."

"You ass, if you took them down you've already read them."

"I took them down, sir, but I did not read them. I never read your private messages, sir."

"Undress me. I want to get into this bath. Then have a vodka brought up to me."

"I'll get it myself."

"No you won't, since you'll be reading those phone messages to me."

"But it's impossible for me to read your phone messages if I'm undressing you."

"Now then, you moron, listen closely. One. You will finish undressing me. Two. Whilst I'm taking a bath and drinking my vodka—at the same time, mind you—you will read me what you wrote down during the time you spent chatting with my friends on the telephone. Now is that so difficult?"

"I do not chat with your friends on the telephone, sir. And I won't be a minute getting you a vodka."

"Look here, Pietro, don't waste any more of my time." Pietro rang downstairs for a vodka. "What did you do that was constructive while I was gone?"

"I took care of your apartment."

"What else?"

"Nothing else."

"What's new in Milan?"

"Nothing."

"My God, the same boring Pietro as ever. I don't pay you to be a wall of silence to *me*, you know." Still nothing. "Did you fix me some hot towels?"

"They're beside the tub, if you'll look, sir."

An Empire table, a Chinese silk screen. On the walls, in defiance of the interior decorator's edicts, Fuseli drawings that miraculously stood up under the steam from the bathtub. Thus far they had, anyway. And two telephones, a reading board across the tub.

"Pietro, fetch me the papers."

"They're right here, sir."

"Read me the headlines while I shave."

"What about the phone messages?"

"Didn't you just get through telling me you didn't want to read them to me?"

"Sir, you ordered me to, therefore I will. However I would like to underline that the ear that listens . . ."

"I know, 'doesn't hear.' Bravo. What do these messages say?"

"One is from the Signora."

"What the hell signora?"

"Your wife, sir. She says she will be arriving on Flight . . ."

"Next message."

"But sir. The Signora will accuse me of not conveying her message. She wanted a car sent."

"Send the car, and anyway she knows her way here perfectly well. Next message."

"The second is from a young lady named Merlina."

"Zerlina."

"I don't think so, since I always ask people to spell their names slowly and carefully so as not to make mistakes."

"Now there you see, you do listen while you're on the phone."

"Not to memorize, just to write down and later pass on."

"Well anyhow, I don't know any Merlinas. I only know Zerlinas."

"Whatever you say, sir. The young lady, whatever her name is, says her phone number is 337-634 and she's in Milan."

"Very good. Don't lose that message, and when you're through reading me the rest of them, dial that number and hand over Miss Merlina."

"You see, I was quite right about her name."

"Next, please."

"Donna Elvira would like you to . . ."

"As you know, I am never at home to that dreary old bore. Next, please."

"The Minister of Commerce wants an appointment to see you tomorrow afternoon, here."

"Call him back and tell him he can come over at seven in the morning."

"Your secretary called to say that your plane will be at Linate airport at 6:30 in the morning. He also said that the bill for the new engine would be . . ."

"Next, please."

"Donna Anna would like to talk to you this afternoon."

"Tell her she can come over around 8."

"A lady from New Zealand called to say she demanded to talk to you."

"If she rings back, give her to me. And take careful notes."

"There's no need. I've a perfect memory."

"Take notes anyway."

"Whatever you say, sir."

"What about my friend the Colonnello?"

"He rang up to ask how you were and if you needed him for anything."

"Ring him back immediately and tell him to get over here on the double."

"Your sister wants you to . . ."

"Which sister?"

"The Marchesa."

"What?"

"What do you mean, 'what'?"

"For Christ's sake, what did my sister the Marchesa want?"

"Oh dear, it slipped my mind to remember her message. Just to show you that what I hear and what I write pass through my mind untouched . . ."

"I don't give a damn what goes on in that mind of

yours. There isn't a thing worth listening to in any of those messages. Ring my sister back and ask her what she wanted."

"Yes, sir. Then the President's private secretary called."

"The President of what?"

"Of the Republic."

"What goddam Republic?"

"Please sir, ours, Italy, the Italian Republic."

"There are plenty of Presidents with private secretaries floating around." He'd finished shaving. "You may now wash my feet."

"But I shan't be able to read you the rest of your messages."

"Seeing as you know them by heart anyway, there's no need to read them."

"But I don't know them by heart. It's as if I'd never heard them before."

"All right, re-read them now, refresh your memory. Then recite them to me while you wash my feet."

"But I've got to concentrate."

"What, on washing my feet?"

"No, on reading the messages, of course."

"You remind me of a Marx brother, I forget which one. All right, what did the President want?"

"It was his secretary, sir."

"If it was the President's secretary, it stands to reason the President wants to tell me something, don't you think?"

"Quite so, sir. He would like to see you tomorrow afternoon at five."

"Call the secretary back and tell him it will have to be at 10 in the morning."

"Where, sir, in Rome?"

"Now where else, the Quirinale isn't in Stockholm, at least not since the last time I was there. I'll take the Minister on board the plane. Therefore change that message and tell him to meet me at Linate airport, 7 A.M. Anything else?"

"Your vodka."

"Ridiculous shaped glass, wouldn't you say, Pietro?"

"Whatever you say, sir."

"Talking to you is the biggest waste of time I know. Hand me the phone, will you, can't you see it's ringing? —You numbskull, what are you doing? Come over immediately." It was the Colonnello. "What do you mean, to do what? We'll find some girls, of course. Not at all, we'll find one for you too . . . Don't act so put upon and get over here in ten minutes . . . What's that you say, you've rung up my poor saintly wife? So that's why she's on her way. Don't you know she can't stand you? Come on, man, get on your horse.—Hang the receiver up."

Ring. "Miss Merlina, sir."

"Dearest Merlina. . . . Of course I remember what your name is, it's just that my idiot butler insists on calling you that. Did you get married? I hope I didn't break up your engagement . . . Good, good, you're a smart girl. Tonight? Marvelous, come round toward 11. Just ask the elevator man to bring you up. I'll be waiting for you. This time I swear Elvira won't barge in. I'm blowing you a kiss for now. Be good."

SCENE TWO

The same

Enter the COLONNELLO

Pietro was drying him off when the Colonnello came in.
"Tell Pietro what you want to drink. What gossip have
you heard?"

"Not a damn thing."

"Another bore. Nobody's had anything interesting to tell
me all day long."

"The Vice President would like to speak with you personally," Pietro said handing him the receiver.

"These pompous asses who think they're too important
to leave a message with the butler. My dear Mr. Vice
President. How good of you to call."

A smile all round, to Pietro and the Colonnello.

I'm well, thank you. *Listen, Giovanni, I've been mean-
ing to talk to you about something that's been on my mind.*
Something's been on your mind, Mr. Vice President? No
I can't possibly see you at seven tomorrow morning. *And
why not?* I never get up before nine. *Make an exception.*
I cannot. *But I must speak with you about this situation.*
Go right ahead. *But it's a delicate question.* I'm alone in
the house. ("Liar," whispered the Colonnello, who was

sitting next to him munching walnuts.) *You can never trust telephones.* That's nothing new, Mr. Vice President. I've known for years that my calls are monitored. What difference does it make? *It makes a great deal of difference to me. Do make an effort and get up a little early tomorrow.* The truth is, Mr. Vice President, I prefer talking over the telephone. *You might have said that before, Giovanni. I wanted to tell you something about an editorial that appeared in one of your newspapers. It can't have escaped your attention.* Probably not. I always try to read all of my newspapers, in spite of there being so many of them. In any case they're the most informative, don't you think? *Well, on occasion they do get a shade out of line.* Really? How's that? *They're verging on the Communistic, my dear Giovanni.* Oh please, Mr. Vice President. Don't make me laugh. After all, who owns them? Was this all you had to say to me? *No. There was one particular editorial which shocked and displeased me.* You've already said that. *In fact, it was a polemic directed personally against me.* No, really? Who signed it? *It wasn't signed.* What was it about? *It seemed well informed regarding certain details, certain top-secret plans.* . . . Very well, Mr. Vice President, I shall look into it and get back to you. *What would you say, Giovanni, if the writer were to publish a retraction.* . . . Something, as I am sure you are quite well aware, Mr. Vice President, that is against my newspapers' policy. My editors and publishers would quit, and where, please, would I find any decent editors and publishers these days? *But there are plenty of bright young men in Italy today.* You say so, you say so, Mr. Vice President. But take my word for it, I'm au courant with the labor situation and I know for a fact that bright young men are few and far between. In fact, I'd even go so far as to say that Italy, today, is jam-packed with one imbecile after another. (He smiled at his audience, happy to have called the Vice President an imbecile in front of the Colonnello and his butler.) *In that case, would you write a letter to your editor?* Brilliant idea. What about? *You could recommend, for example . . .* Yes? *That the letter I write be printed.* But we publish all Letters to the Editor. *Well then. Perhaps you can give me some assurance that the writer won't answer my letter.* But why? If your letter is a protest against false information, then the writer will have to defend his statements. *Now look here, Giovanni, bit by bit I'm getting the impression that you wrote that editorial yourself.* But Mr. Vice President, everybody knows I'm illiterate. As if I had the time to write articles denouncing people like you. But if you want to go on with this discussion, meet me at Linate airport tomorrow morning at 6:30. My plane will bring you back to Milan after it's dropped me off in Rome. Nice to talk to you, bye.

"What did the Vice President have to say for himself?" (*Colonnello*)

"As if you weren't listening. You know, he's very sweet, though. Imagine having the face to ring up for a thing like that."

"Donna Anna on the phone." (*Pietro*)

"Jesus Christ." (*Colonnello, worried*)

Dearest Anna. We must be brief because I've got a senator with me who went out of his way to come. *I've been dying to talk to you, Giovanni.* Well then, go ahead. *May I come by today?* But I told Pietro you could come

around 8. *Who's Pietro?* My butler. *Ottavio must not find
out* . . . What, don't tell me my butler is related to your
husband? *Look, it's not a bit funny.* ("Sir, your sister is on
the other wire.") Which sister? Oh, I beg your pardon,
Anna. *What was that you said?* I said, which sister. *I don't
have any sisters.* I know you don't, but I've got hordes of
them. *Look, I didn't ring you up to have you pull my leg.*
The Marchesa? Hand her over. Listen Anna, bye and see
you later. *All right, but I'm not a Marchesa.* Good lord,
another witless woman, she'll wind up being an eternal
nuisance too. Pietro, a little while after she gets here, you
come into the living room. If we haven't gone off to bed,
inform me that I have an important phone call and must
leave immediately. ("Will you please tell me why you
dragged me over here, since you clearly plan to spend the
night talking on the telephone?"—*Colonnello*) To hold
my hand, of course. No, no, not you, lovey, I was talking to
the Colonnello. *Don't tell me you still run around with that
idiot.* He's not the idiot he seems. And besides, lovey, time
and again I've told you, you have your friends and I'll
have mine. You're worse than Mother used to be. *There
you go shooting your mouth off again, I suppose the
Colonnello heard every word.* How could he possibly, he's
sitting right here next to me eating nuts, walnuts in fact.
*Listen, my dear brother, one of your foulmouthed news-
papers is about to print an obscene article about my cousin.*
Why obscene? *For the simple reason that my cousin behaves obscenely.* Lovey, you can't blame me for the way
your cousin behaves. *But certainly you can't get any
pleasure out of printing gossip columns devoted to your
own relatives.* All right, lovey, which paper is it? *Domani.*

But it's already out on the stands. *I know that.* Be reasonable, lovey duck, we'll have to withdraw the entire issue. *You're a dear, you know. When will we see you? Why don't you visit us this summer? You're never around.* I know, it's because I've got too damn much to do, picking up behind our obscene family. *Bye, dear.*

"Pietro. Ring up Macchi and tell him if that column on my cousin comes out, I'll have his head."

"But he won't be at the office at this hour."

"Find out his home number and give him the message immediately. You don't suppose I pay you to do easy things like wash my feet, do you? Now then. Colonnello. Shall we go out for a drink?"

SCENE THREE

A hotel bar

DON GIOVANNI, the COLONNELLO

"That Pietro's a sly old fox. He pretends to be completely mindless, but I know he's sharp as a tack. What do you think of him?"

"I've never really paid much attention to him."

"You should. He's one of my servants just like you."

"I am not one of your servants."

Among steady customers at our hotel we are proud to number the Hon. Don Giovanni, who is photographed here having a drink in our Golden Room.

Don Giovanni and friend having cocktails in a downtown hotel.

As you can see, prominent personalities drink our product.

The prince of wristwatches is worn by the men who rule the world: royalty, Presidents, politicians, generals.

Men of good taste ask for . . .

Join this glittering group now, buy . . .

The best clothes are made by . . .

Men's styles by . . .

According to some unwritten law of hotel management, fake rococo plus threadbare satin equals luxury. Well, what can you do. Ahah. Over there, a pretty girl. Short short hair, delicate neck, fine lips.

"She looks like a model."

"The trouble with models is, when you get them home, three-quarters of them start peeling off false eyelashes, wigs, padded breasts, half-an-inch-thick makeup, and in the end there's nothing left to screw."

The girl spotted Don Giovanni watching her. She smiled. The bartender wasn't sure who the unknown beauty was, but he figured it was worth something to Don Giovanni that the girl's companion, just hidden by the booth wall, was Donna Elvira. Well, well. But even that wasn't enough to make him give up that nice smile.

"Colonnello, be a good boy and run over there and find out what those two are saying to each other."

They were going to a masked ball Trazom was giving, the Colonnello reported after eavesdropping for ten minutes. The model was masquerading as a siren and Elvira as Circe. "You're sure, the enchantress Circe?" Yes, Elvira was dressing as Circe. "My God, she couldn't charm the smoke out of a fire."

"Circe turned men into pigs."

"Nitpicker. Now listen to me, Colonnello. I've a splendid idea."

"I'm starving."

"You're always starving. Go on and eat."

"I will, thanks."

"Now then. We're going to Cesarino's ball, dressed in plumed hats. But you dress as me, and I'll vice versa. You woo Circe the pig and I'll make the siren. We'll have a smashing time. Tell Elvira you've always loved her."

"Who, me?"

"Dolt. At that point, you're masquerading as *me.*"

"What about my voice?"

"Make an effort and change it. Anyway she'll be crocked and all worked up. Everything will happen fast, in the dark, in monosyllables."

"Poor thing."

"I didn't ask for your opinion."

"You know what Elvira was telling the model? That she still loves you."

"What tripe to tell people. Obviously she had nothing more interesting to say."

Giovanni sent Pietro out to buy black cloaks and masks. A milliner set to work immediately to cover two huge felt hats with plumes.

INTERMISSION

Milan, STAFF EXCLUSIVE. —Cesarino Trazom has become a powerful man in a very few years, with the help of prominent Italian politicians and private citizens, among them Commander E. Acciaiuoli, deceased yesterday in Naples.

This evening Trazom will inaugurate his new Milan Center (popularly called "Cesarino's Pleasure Dome") with a masked ball. The Center has been described as one of the most sumptuous buildings in Milan. The ceiling and walls of the grand entranceway are black marble. The floor is excavated with pools containing sculptures of nymphs and nereids.

Informed observers report that paths of smooth cobblestones wind among the pools, providing water-free walkways. The receptionist's desk, made of soapstone, is surrounded by papyrus plants. It "springs" from the water, as does the porter's booth, which is decorated with conch shells.

Knowledgeable sources say there will be music everywhere, pitched at the exact frequency to absorb the noise of humidifiers and airconditioners. The top floor, which offers a stunning panorama of our city, houses the directorial offices as well as a hanging garden full of tropical plants and statues depicting Trazom's various benefactors.

Informed observers also noted a small pool filled with mercury, said to have cost the industrialist as much again as the entire building. A specially constructed network of steel girders was installed to support the weight of the mercury-filled tank.

Trazom claims it is the only pool of its kind in the world.

Before entering the president's private office, observers say, one passes through the administrative council's conference room. The Milan vista is hidden behind panels reproducing it in an expressionistic cyclorama, the work of a noted Ligurian artist.

A second wall consists of blue glass behind which gambol red and blue tropical fish. Trazom believes the movement of the water and fish to be relaxants.

The industrialist's office houses the largest desk in Europe, apart from the original of which it is a copy, to be found in the Wallace Museum, London. Black leather Barcelona chairs are provided for visitors. Eleven telephones are to be seen in the office, six of which are interoffice.

This is the only skyscraper to be erected in the city of Milan over which no social protest was aroused. Trazom is among other things the intimate friend of the prominent industrialist and newspaper magnate Don Giovanni. He is the owner of various Rolls-Royces, Aston Martins, and two Ferraris, all of which contain telephones.

Our informants say that more than 600 persons will attend the ball inaugurating Trazom's Center this evening.

SCENE FOUR

DON GIOVANNI

You're a son-of-a-bitch, giving a ball and forgetting to invite me. Louder, I can't hear a word you're saying . . . Working hard my eye, you've got some girl you're balling up there in your office, I can tell. Already inaugurated your new building, eh? I mean sexually. . . . Oh for God's sake, I hope your secretary does hear every word I'm saying. Is she pretty, your secretary? What, she's a man? Well, that's a new twist. Listen, what are you wearing tonight? . . . Well, Cesarino, actually I called to ask you to do me a favor. I'm dressing up as the Colonnello—yes, I still "run round with him," my God, you're worse than my sister. Anyway, he's putting on my clothes, just masks and hats. I want you to tell Donna Elvira that I confided in you, that I told you that, well, I'm in love with her. Then escort her over to the Colonnello and introduce him as me . . . Bravo, perfect. Business? Oh, business is booming, of course I'm not quite so ostentatious as you about it . . . See you later.

He tried to get hold of Zerlina but she wasn't home. He left a message to meet him at Trazom's ball and that he would be a little late getting there.

SCENE FIVE

The living room of Giovanni's penthouse

DONNA ANNA, *later* DON GIOVANNI

Anna was sitting on the couch, smoking and thumbing through magazines. Giovanni was late. She flipped through the pages.

VIETNAMESE PROSTITUTE IN BAR

VIETNAMESE PROSTITUTE IN BOOTH IN RED-LIGHT DISTRICT

The principal national industry has become prostitution.

Prostitutes' rates range from 50 piasters to a maximum of 3,000. Everything from cheap bordellos to luxury hotels serviced by call girls can be seen springing up and thriving.

There are 14,000 houses of ill repute. (*flip*)

PROSTITUTE FROM THE TAN QUARTER WITH VIETNAMESE PROSTITUTE

GIRLS BEING REGISTERED (*flip*)

PHOTO TAKEN JUST AFTER DOCTOR'S EXAMINATION

VENEREAL DISEASES (*flip*)

HARD-TO-CURE CASES (*flip*)

THE YOUNG G I'S FRUSTRATION

FORBIDDEN SAIGON (*flip*)

Left: OPEN-AIR WHOREHOUSE
Right: BROTHEL IN RED-LIGHT DISTRICT (*flip*)
Average rates for prostitutes are . . . (*flip flip*)
Prostitution increases at a daily rate of . . . (*flip*)
TENDERNESS IN A HOUSE OF PROSTITUTION

The magazines were getting to be wholly unreadable these days. You'd think Giovanni would make his own publications a little less morose.

The door had opened.

"Giovanni."

"How are you?"

"Fine, very well, thank you."

He embraced her tightly and kissed her on the mouth without batting an eye. His hands under her armpits, he was always after the same thing.

"You mustn't do that, after what's happened."

"Now, now, don't tease me." Still embraced.

"I came to tell you that Ottavio is out to avenge the family honor." His hand toyed with her breast and his lips nibbled at her cheek.

"You told him about us?" One of these days he would find a female who could keep her mouth shut.

"No, he just suspects. He says you brought on my father's stroke." His mouth vaguely on hers and one eye watching her.

"*I* did?"

"He's right, you know." He squeezed her thighs and pressed them up against his. Anna could feel the shape of his legs. And of his desire.

"Absurd. Obviously your father had a weak heart and

would have died anyway. The very next day at the latest. If every father who caught his daughter in flagrante dropped dead, Italy would be full of corpses and orphans."

"Giovanni, don't make fun of things like that." He laughed against her ear and Anna closed her eyes.

"Nobody ever tells the truth about the dead."

"Are you insinuating that I . . ." He was fondling her hair now, his hand against her neck.

"No, I wasn't speaking specifically of you."

"I was his only daughter and he idolized me." He had taken hold of her shoulders and was pressing her breasts to him.

"Not a very prolific man. How does Ottavio plan to wreak his vengeance on me?"

"He wants to frighten you to death." He'd got his hand under her blouse and unfastened her brassière. He was playing with her breast, massaging it. Anna felt her blood churning.

"If I were you, dearest Anna, I wouldn't let it worry me. My heart's in good shape and I'm very brave. I've never been afraid of anything in my life."

"He might kill you." He held one breast between his fingers while he lifted off her blouse with the other hand.

"He'd have to spend the rest of his life in a dungeon."

"He'd do it for love of me." His hands found their way down to her stomach and Anna couldn't resist the pleasure they gave her. Her insides melted.

"For just that reason he wouldn't do it. It's clear he likes going to bed with you and if he had to go to prison he couldn't any more. And he's got a point. Come on, let's do it too."

She followed him. Anna noted with relief that a carved

crucifix reigned over Giovanni's immense bed. And a votive light on the bureau confirmed his faith. *He too is a believer, Father. Will God have mercy on us?* ALL THE SECRETS OF YOUR DREAMS FINALLY REVEALED IN

The Book of Dreams
The Seer of Your Future
and the Path to Follow
to Good Fortune

Dear Countess Beatrice. I write to you in desperation for advice. I have fallen in love with a true believer, but he has no morals. My husband, who is entirely faithful to his marital vows, does not know about it. My confessor disapproves. Nevertheless I am fatally attracted by this man and all my thoughts are always on him. I cannot forget him, and the more I think about him, the more my husband's company becomes distasteful to me. What should I do?
　　　　　　　　　　　　—Soul in Torment, Naples

Dear Soul in Torment: You didn't tell me how long you've been married or how old you are. These troubles of the heart, I am duty-bound to tell you, are passing fancies, youthful folly. And perfectly normal!! After five or six years of marriage, these things happen to everyone. But: be strong. Don't surrender to the man who fascinates you so. Seek the counsel of your Father Confessor often, and I advise you to take a short trip alone with your husband.

"Are you religious?"

"What a question to ask. I'm Catholic like every other Italian."

"Not every other Italian is Catholic."

"Precisely my point."

Conversation with Anna was enough to put you to

sleep. Anyway he was eager to get it over with fast. There she was, already half naked, her rich, beautiful, white breasts uncovered. Exciting, that body chopped in half by a garter belt. There was something vaguely sordid and stimulating about a half-naked woman. Anna started to take off her stockings. He stopped her. He wanted her as she was. And began to take her avidly, as if he couldn't get enough of her. Anna was in a trance. She kissed Giovanni and the medal that hung by a chain from his neck, an image of the Virgin. Anna. His hands traveling roughly through her hair . . . finally in his eagerness he dislodged her wig and found himself holding her hair in his hands. How off-putting. In fact, how downright disgusting. "Models and actresses at least have the decency to take them off before they get in bed."

Anna in her amorous trance didn't realize what had happened. It seemed to her a thunderbolt from Heaven, a reproof direct from God, a total condemnation.

"Come on, let's bathe." Giovanni took account of her thorough chagrin and shock.

Anna rabid, lying on the bed half naked.

INCLUDES FREE GIFT BOOKLET

LOVE'S TALISMAN. Success and happiness in LOVE. For the buyers of our specialties, a gift: Prof. Duke Black's invaluable book, fully illustrated with photographs and drawings. *For men:* Tells how to be irresistible, how to conquer women, how to banish self-consciousness, how to become robust and handsome, how to succeed in business and in affairs of the heart. *For women:* Tells how to be beautiful and fascinating, desired and loved; how to make yourself loved by your loved one, how to be elegant, how to have pliant, velvety skin, how to write beautiful love letters.

ARVID SCIENTIFIC RESEARCH INSTITUTE INC.

To Baron Gottfried von Jacquin
                                    Prague, 15–25 October 1787
    . . . Now Don Giovanni is scheduled for the 24th.
    . . . The 21st. It was scheduled for the 24th, but they've postponed it again due to the illness of one of the singers. Since the company is so small, the impresario is in a continual state of anxiety and has to keep to himself as much as possible since it might even be that some unforeseen indisposition will push him into the strangest of situations, that is, of having no spectacle at all to present . . .
                                    Wolfgang Mozart.

                                    Vienna, 19 December 1787
Dearest Sister,
    . . . Probably you have already heard that I have written Don Giovanni and that the opera was a triumphant success, but that His Imperial Majesty has commanded me to serve him is doubtless news to you . . .
                                    Wolfgang Amadeus.

SCENE SIX

The same

Enter PIETRO

It was getting late. Giovanni rang and Pietro zoomed in without knocking, eliciting a scream of horror from Anna. Her wig between her knees, her breasts bare, there was nothing nearby to cover her in haste.

"Now don't fly into a tizzy. It's only the butler." In fact, Pietro hadn't so much as glanced at her.

"Get him out of here instantly."

"But I rang for him."

Pietro dragged out a couple of bathrobes. Anna, now nominally covered by the sheet, was trying to fix her wig.

"You know, you look perfectly attractive in short hair."

"Do let's not harp on the subject."

Don Giovanni had the strangest sensation that the wig accident had upset Anna more than her father's death.

He was right. And Anna was planning her revenge.

Pietro avoided looking at Anna, whose right breast kept popping out of the folds of the sheet.

"Sir, your bath is ready."

"Good."

"Sir, while you were otherwise occupied, Judge Sanvitali rang up."

Anna covered her face with the sheet, in the process exposing her left breast. This had never happened before: her presence ignored, her body exposed, the butler, the wig.

"The Colonnello has arrived, sir."

"Tell him to wait in the library."

"Giovanni, can I get out of here without running into the Colonnello too?"

"You'll have to wait until after we leave."

Giovanni in his perfumed bath. He took three or four during the day, all very short, all scented with expensive bath salts. His handsome body, his well-developed musculature. This class of people he simply could not abide; this Anna and her mindless hypocrisy. Even movie stars were better: they were whores and made no bones about it. The men were all bandits. The same was true of politics and industry. At least there you knew who you were talking to. But this woman was patently a waste of time. Just another whimpering bore.

"How are you doing?"

"Were you talking to me?" Anna's icy voice.

"Come in here."

"But you're undressed."

"You've seen me undressed often enough."

She was even crying now. Another Elvira in the making, definitely. It was like a recurring nightmare.

"You rang, sir?" Pietro asked. He took in the bedroom, which contained only Anna in tears, and went into the bathroom.

"Dress me."

Anna tried to make herself invisible while Pietro dressed Don Giovanni before her very eyes. Don Giovanni had made love to her and offended her in the most unforgivable way possible.

SCENE SEVEN

Trazom Industrial Center

DON GIOVANNI, the COLONNELLO, SIREN, DONNA ELVIRA, TRAZOM, GUESTS *in costume*

Masqueraders out of breath from trying to keep to the cobblestones and avoid falling into the pools. Here and there, crushed papyrus, the casualty of some graceless woman.

Most of the guests went directly to the top floor, primarily to get out of range of the waiters scurrying around on the cobblestone paths balancing trays precariously.

Trazom recognized Don Giovanni immediately in spite of his plumes and mask and went over to say hello. Trazom was dressed as the Sun King.

"How catastrophic," Don Giovanni commented. "I mustn't look a bit like the Colonnello."

"Don't be silly, you look fine. Don't lose heart. In any

case, I've never met a woman yet with an eye for detail when she was out of her mind with bliss."

"When you come right down to it, no woman has an eye for detail, out of her mind with bliss or not."

"You're absolutely wrong, listen to them talk about each other some time. It's only when it comes to us that they haven't any eyes at all."

INTERMISSION

DONNA ELVIRA
It was a ghastly debacle. You've no idea how thoroughly they humiliated me. The Colonnello, disguised as Don Giovanni, took me to one side and dragged me off with him.

DON OTTAVIO
Where?

DONNA ELVIRA
Into some office. What could I do? He didn't say much, I was a bit tipsy, I was blissful of course. And I was convinced it was Giovanni.

DON OTTAVIO
So what went on in the office?

DONNA ELVIRA
Really, must you ask questions of the sort. What do you

suppose went on? Precisely what you're thinking, of course. And on top of a desk to boot.

DON OTTAVIO
What about Don Giovanni?

DONNA ELVIRA
He in the meanwhile made off with a friend of mine, a model. That was even more horrendous. Oh really, I can't go on.

DON OTTAVIO
Please do continue.

DONNA ELVIRA
Even Masetto showed up. He found a note at Zerlina's telling her to meet Giovanni at Trazom's. Masetto was determined to throttle Giovanni: of course it wound up with Giovanni breaking Masetto's nose.

DON OTTAVIO
And then?

DONNA ELVIRA
And then Zerlina turned up to nurse poor Masetto, whom she found on the floor holding his head in his hands, whimpering. You know how young couples are, they shut themselves into an office and turned off all the lights. The lord knows what they were doing when I came in with the man I thought was Giovanni. Really the most hateful practical joke. Horrid. Humiliating. Degrading.

DON OTTAVIO
   Yes, cruel. Do go on.

DONNA ELVIRA
   Masetto recognized the man who'd beaten him up in
the dark, that is Don Giovanni, I mean the Colonnello—
well, anyway, he was about to attack my companion when
you came in. Now what were you doing at Trazom's?

DON OTTAVIO
   Well, to tell the truth, I'd noticed that Anna has been
acting a little strange towards me lately, so I decided to
call in a detective agency.* I was informed that Anna had
been to visit Don Giovanni and that she was going to
Trazom's ball. See, you can't even trust private detectives.
My dear Anna, as you saw, arrived after he did, all fresh
and innocent.

DONNA ELVIRA
   We must punish Don Giovanni. And make him repent.
But what would work?

DON OTTAVIO
   Look, Don Giovanni is upstairs in the hanging gardens
right at this moment. You know there are several statues
up there, among them one of Commander Acciaiuoli. If I
hide behind that statue and start intoning in a deep voice,
Giovanni will die of fright. The dark, the statues barely lit
up, a creepy voice—the place will seem full of ghosts. Don
Giovanni will beg for mercy and repent.

* *See page 154.*

SCENE EIGHT

A terrace vegetated with tropical plants and marble statues

DON GIOVANNI, *later* the COLONNELLO

He was just about to leave when he saw the Colonnello come in. He was in a lather and muttering to himself.

"What are you doing?"

"Who's there?"

"Don't tell me you don't recognize yourself."

"Ah, it's you. I hope you're aware that because of you I was almost murdered by all those horrid people."

"You should feel honored to have been taken for me. So tell me, how did you make out with Elvira?"

"That part went off exactly according to plan."

Giovanni's laughter rose from his mouth to his eyes and then drifted down to his belly.

A weird rumble, gloomy, cavernous.

"Who's that?"

"It's just your stomach grumbling, moron."

"It wasn't either. I just ate something a few minutes ago."

"Then it's somebody pulling our leg." Giovanni was right the second time round. "Colonnello, skip over there and see if that isn't the statue of the Commander."

Again, the eerie growling, which seemed to be saying something. The Colonnello shivered with fear.

"I wouldn't dream of going over there."

"Did anybody ever tell you, you're pure chicken? Come on, walk over there and ask that goddam statue to dinner. It's de rigeur in situations like this."

"Be serious, will you. Look at that statue, it seems to be moving. It's speaking again. Damn it, man, I'm frightened. Look, it nodded its head. It accepts your invitation. Good Christ, Holy Mother, it *is* the Commander's statue, it looks just like him. In fact it looks alive. Enough to be breathing. Jesus Mary, I've never seen anything like it. Listen . . . he says . . . he talked . . . he says he's coming to dinner. Come on, let's get the hell out of here. *Right now.*"

SCENE NINE

A room in Don Giovanni's penthouse

DON GIOVANNI, PIETRO

"Pietro."

"Yes, sir?"

"Fix dinner."

"At this hour?"

"Nobody asked your opinion."

"For two?"

"Very good, how did you guess? I'm expecting a gentleman."

"Then it will have to be for three."

"I don't understand."

"There's a young lady here."

"What's her name?"

"Miss Merlina, sir."

"Quite right, I'd forgotten about her. Miss Merlina indeed. All right, set for three then."

"What about me?" (*Colonnello*)

"You ate before we went to Trazom's and while we were there."

"I'd be glad to eat again with you."

"You can keep Pietro company and help him out."

"That's rather uncivil of you."

"I was under the impression a moment ago that you were terrified of the Commander's statue."

"Well, if there are going to be a lot of us . . ."

"There aren't going to be a lot of us. There will be three of us. So make yourself scarce for a while, will you."

SCENE TEN

The same

Enter ZERLINA

"Dear little Zerlina."

"You're late."

"Sorry, something cropped up. And something else is

just about to: we're having company for dinner. But we'll get rid of the guest afterward."

"Who's this guest?"

"I'm not exactly sure. Can you stay the night?"

"Of course."

"You were right not to come to Trazom's. It was deadly dull."

"But I did go."

"Really? I didn't see you there."

"I'm not quite clear on what happened, but perhaps I'd best not pry."

"What do you mean?"

"Well, first of all, which of you beat up Masetto? Then, Donna Elvira thought she was with you when actually she was with the Colonnello. Ottavio was out to kill you because he thought his wife had been with you. However Donna Anna showed up alone and was clearly looking for you. Then they all got together and decided to get even."

"Really? How?"

"Ottavio wanted to put on a ghost show. Hide behind a statue and scare the living daylights out of you."

"A ghost?"

"Yes, Commander Acciaiuoli's, of all people."

"Who's safely up in Heaven, if I can believe my own newspapers."

"They were deadly serious, you know, they're really out to get you."

"Punish me? For what?"

"I wouldn't know."

"What about you, do you want to punish me too?"

"Who, me? Nothing could be further from my mind."
She embraced him and closed her eyes against his cheek.

"Dear little Zerlina . . . How old are you?"

"Old enough to. What about you?"

"Mature."

"Are you?"

"What?"

"Mature."

"Mature enough for what?"

"You were talking about maturity . . . I imagine you meant understanding life, situations, people . . ."

"What are you babbling about? That's stuff you read in books and just as meaningless. Don't you agree? Do you read a lot?"

"Some. What about you?"

"Books bore me."

"My, my, so much bores you. Doubtless that's why all these things happen to you."

"What do you mean?"

"You cause them to happen. You bring them down on your own head."

"Tonight you're just full of ideas, aren't you. Listen, I'm dying for you. I haven't yet been able to . . ."

"I know, somebody always comes bumbling in. Tonight, even, this guest is coming to dinner."

SCENE ELEVEN

The same, later the Brown Room

Enter PIETRO *and the* COLONNELLO

"Good evening, miss."

"Good evening."

"Dinner is served."

"What lovely pictures."

"Do you like them? That one's new. I bought it three days ago in New York. Colonnello. I told you you weren't to eat with us. Can't you see the table's only set for three?"

"Who's the third?" Zerlina asked again.

"But Giovanni, you don't really believe that ghost is going to accept your invitation?"

"He'd be a fool not to. How many ghosts get invited to apartments like this?"

"Listen, it's nothing to kid about."

"In fact, I'll even go so far as to say the ghost would be damned unmannerly not to turn up. You and Pietro serve the dinner."

"I've never served table."

"Then turn on the television."

"The television?"

"See if there's anything entertaining on. I want to hear the news."

"But you're the one that's always saying the newscaster never has any news."

"Then let's have a bit of the Pope. Let's see if we can get something as amusing as *Humanae Vitae* out of him this week."

"What makes you think the Pope will be on?"

"Because my hot line to God tells me so. Jesus, Colonnello, as if the case weren't that the Pope is always on Italian television. And keep your hands out of the food."

"What do you mean?"

"I saw you filching food. You've still got some in your mouth."

"I was hungry."

"You're insatiable. Zerlina, please help yourself."

"Aren't we waiting for this famous third party, then?"

The door opened.

"Here he is."

Instead Pietro came in.

"Donna Elvira is here."

INTERMISSION

Prague, EXCLUSIVE.—Observers and musicians concur in the opinion that there has never been anything like this in Prague. Maestro Mozart himself conducted. Upon entering the pit, he was greeted by a standing ovation.

The opera is severely taxing on musicians and singers alike. Nevertheless the company is to be complimented on the splendid production, which was put together practically overnight.

The cast and orchestra, in fact all concerned, delivered up some of the best performances of their careers to

Maestro Mozart in one of the most remarkable evenings in musical memory.

The capacity house was delirious and the opera promises to remain a long time in our repertory.

Seated in the parterre was M. Jacques Casanova, who made a special trip to Prague for the première of *Don Giovanni,* from his retirement villa at Dux.

SCENE TWELVE

The same

Enter DONNA ELVIRA

"I'm imagining it. Madam Bad Penny. It can't be her again." He was wrong. It was unquestionably Donna Elvira. "My dear Elvira, you seem distraught. What are you doing all dressed up as a pi—I mean to say, as Circe?"

"Do you mean to tell me, Giovanni, that you weren't at that ball?"

"What ball?"

"Giovanni. This joke, which is in the worst imaginable taste, has gone far enough. I've come to give you one last chance to recognize your obligations towards me."

"Obligations? What is it you want from me?"

"Your penitence."

"You have it."

"You ogre."

"Will you leave me in peace. If you like, I'll have a place set and you can join us for supper. Then, in about an hour, you will please depart and don't come back or start with the endless phone calls again."

Elvira stumbled toward the door in tears. A chilling shriek. The Colonnello choked on his wine and Zerlina shuddered.

"What is going on in this apartment? Colonnello. Go see what's happened. That bitch is always trying to kill herself."

The Colonnello went out. A shout of horror, this time the Colonnello's voice. A knock was heard at the door. Pietro dropped his tray.

SCENE THIRTEEN

The same

Enter STATUE OF COMMANDER

"Did you hear that?"

"Someone's knocking, that's all. Go let him in."

"Oooh, I'm scared." Zerlina smiled to herself, realizing that they were about to see Ottavio's mise-en-scène. The door opened of its own accord and the room was plunged into darkness. The candle flames gave off the only light, reflected in the plates and glasses. The silk curtains rustled in somber sworls. There the statue was, poised in the doorway. Towering like a pillar, wrapped in a phosphorescent white cloak. Clouds of smoke billowed up around it. Its face was surrounded by tiny blue tongues of fire. Quick currents of cold air flitted into the room and Zerlina felt her legs chill. "It's only Ottavio," she whispered to Giovanni.

"Brilliantly staged. He's very good, don't you think?"

"Don Giovanni," the cavernous voice intoned. "I have come to you. I have accepted your invitation, and here you see me before you."

"I certainly do see you before me, and I couldn't have hoped for more. Colonnello, Pietro. Serve the Commander immediately."

"Sir, I'm petrified," Pietro squeaked from behind a curtain.

The Colonnello, who'd wound up under the dinner table, couldn't utter anything at all for his chattering teeth.

"Do not move," the voice went on ominously. Every time it spoke, vapors rose up and the room got colder. Suddenly the candles blew out. "Wait."

"He must have an airconditioner tucked away under that sheet," Don Giovanni whispered to Zerlina.

"Hear me now, Don Giovanni." A voice like God in a Cecil B. De Mille Bible epic. It echoed off the walls. The cold, the dark.

"I'm all ears." To Zerlina, in a whisper, "If this keeps up, you and I aren't going to bed tonight either."

"*Hear me now, Don Giovanni!*" A dense cloud of white smoke enveloped the table. Frigid.

"You don't have to shout, I'm listening."

"You invited me to dinner."

"You already said that. My, my, aren't ghosts repetitive these days."

"Then you know your duty. Will you accept my invitation? Will you dine with me?"

"He's awfully busy, he couldn't possibly." (*Colonnello, from under the table*)

"Mind your own damn business. I've never had dinner with a ghost. I'd be delighted."

The vapor clouded up the glasses and the window panes. The plates were brimming with cold water and even the linen had icicles clinging to it.

"Give me your word."

"Damn it, man, I just told you I'd come. What do you want, a contract?"

Now even Zerlina was frightened. The sham was so well done that it seemed completely plausible. The blue flames and the statue's white cloak were blinding. And the cold was fast becoming intolerable. The beads of water on the glasses had frozen.

"Give me your hand on it."

"Now he's gone too far. If I get that close, I'll be able to see perfectly well that it's Ottavio." But he got up and walked over to the statue.

"Help! My God, the cold! What horrible hands you have!"

"Repent," the statue intoned, "before your time runs out."

"Don't be absurd, why should I repent?"

"Repent, I say!"

"No!"

"You have no more time." Flames lept out of the Aubusson carpet. A thunderclap. Voices, hideous hissing.

"What a monster you are! And this ice. Will you be good enough to let go of my hand, please?"

Finally Don Giovanni gave out a howl of anguish and vanished into the smoke. At once the lights went on and the temperature rose to normal. But Don Giovanni and the statue had disappeared.

FINALE

The same

DONNA ELVIRA, the COLONNELLO, ZERLINA, DON OTTAVIO, DONNA ANNA, MASETTO

Elvira staggered back in, pale with fear.

"Where did he go?"

Enter Don Ottavio, followed by Donna Anna and Masetto.

"What's going on here?"

"But wasn't it you under the sheet?" (*Zerlina, astounded*)

"Sheet? What sheet? We just got here. We were about to appear as a ghost."

"Well then?"

"Well then, what?"

"Are you quite sure it wasn't you, Don Ottavio?"

"What wasn't me? Will somebody please tell me what's going on."

"Dressed up like a statue, dragging him off . . ."

"Who, me? Dragging who off? Don Giovanni? I did no such thing."

"The ice . . . the smoke . . . his screams . . . that voice . . ." the Colonnello chattered out.

"Well, now what are we going to do?" asked Elvira, looking around.

"I couldn't even hazard a guess," said the Colonnello. "Particularly since without him, I haven't anything at all to do."

"What about me?" Zerlina asked. "I'll be bored to death. And we never even . . ."

"What about me?" Masetto glared at Zerlina. "Being jealous of him beat hell out of fighting off the usual assholes who come after you."

"Assuming I don't retire to a convent," Elvira put in, "I'll be condemned to wander around Europe pointlessly. Up to now, my purpose in life was hunting for Don Giovanni. I didn't mind only catching glimpses of him once or twice a month. Even when I knew perfectly well he'd never take me back. I suppose I might as well really kill myself this time."

"Actually it's much sadder than that for me," Donna Anna thought aloud. "I truly loved the man. And without him, what excuse can I give Ottavio for not going to bed with him?"

"And what other excuse could I accept from you? In fact, Anna, now that he's gone I feel much less in love with you. It was rather a source of pride to me, his wanting to go to bed with you."

"Perhaps we should all avenge ourselves on Commander Acciaiuoli?" the Colonnello suggested.

"No, we can't do that," Donna Anna objected. "After all, he's my father, and besides, he's already dead."

In despair, they all began to cry.

Now what ever gave all those people the absurd idea that a ghost would be invulnerable to Don Giovanni's charms?

Because, incidentally, the two did not descend into Hell. Instead Don Giovanni took the Commander's ghost on board his private plane, where they began a lengthy debate about the problems of modern industry. Afterward they boarded a swift yacht that took them to beautiful, unexploited tropical islands.

There they remain to this day, immortal throughout eternity.

Which is Don Giovanni's punishment: to be immortal, to live out eternity with a man, and to be bored to tears.